I0459531

MISSING IN MICHIGAN

Alexa Bentley Paranormal Mysteries Book One

April A. Taylor

Missing in Michigan: Alexa Bentley Paranormal Mysteries Book One Copyright © 2018 by April A. Taylor. All Rights Reserved.

All rights reserved. No part of this book may be reproduced in any form or by any electronic or mechanical means including information storage and retrieval systems, without permission in writing from the author. The only exception is by a reviewer, who may quote short excerpts in a review.

Cover designed by OliviaProDesign

This book is a work of fiction. Names, characters, places, and incidents either are products of the author's imagination or are used fictitiously. Any resemblance to actual persons, living or dead, events, or locales is entirely coincidental.

April A. Taylor
Visit my website at www.AprilATaylor.net

Printed in the United States of America

First Printing: June 2018
Midnight Grasshopper Books

BIBLIOGRAPHY

<u>Alexa Bentley Paranormal Mysteries</u>

Book One – Missing in Michigan
Book Two – Frightened in France
Book Three – Lost in Louisiana (COMING SOON!)

<u>Midnight Myths and Fairy Tales Series</u>

Book One – Vasilisa the Terrible: A Baba Yaga Story
Book Two – Death Song of the Sea: A Celtic Story

<u>Horror</u>

The Haunting of Cabin Green: A Modern Gothic Horror Novel

REVIEWS

Alexa Bentley Paranormal Mysteries

"I love Alex! She's the witty, sometimes snarky, definitely quirky best friend you didn't know you needed." – Goodreads Reviewer

"The author's voice is fresh and inviting. I was intrigued from beginning to end! I honestly can't wait till book 2." – Goodreads Reviewer

Midnight Myths and Fairy Tales

"Beautifully bewitching... it's a fast-paced, captivating tale, and the writing is exquisite." – Kindle Reviewer

The Haunting of Cabin Green

"This was a very interesting psychological thriller... It reminded me of a Stephen King Novel. Taylor did a fantastic job on her detail of the eerie experiences that become Ben's reality." – N.M. McGregor, Author of The Montana Series

This book is for every quirky, witty, sassy woman who helped inspire the character of Alexa Bentley, ranging from old friends to a hilarious cashier at Kroger. Keep being you, ladies

CHAPTER ONE

My name is Alexa Bentley, but you can call me Alex. I'm also what you might call a ghost therapist. Think that sounds like a bunch of woo? I did too, until I didn't.

Do you believe all our cares simply melt away and our soul soars weightless after death? I hate to break it to you, but everyone you've ever loved and lost still has all the same baggage. And in some cases, dying makes it even worse.

The hardest part for me is when they don't know their life is over. Imagine having to tell a powerfully psychotic killer that he's dead. Or how about telling a devoted mother she can no longer help her children? It gets messy. And when things get messy in the spirit world, humans often pay a steep price.

That brings us to today. There's a good reason I'm lying flat on my ass in the dusty attic of an old Victorian home in Baltimore. The ghost I'm currently trying to counsel is *not* taking it well.

I steel myself against the inevitable next assault and raise my head. "I'm very sorry for your loss. But you're scaring your wife. Is that really what you want?"

The ghost's cold eyes consider me. Spirits don't look like people envision, at least not to me. Where you might see nothing at all or just the slightest wisp of a darkened outline, I see them as they once were. But even the kindest, most gregarious ghosts often become a hardened version of their former selves. Unfortunately for me, there's nothing kind about this one.

A blast of air engulfs my body as a roar of anguish escapes his spectral lips. I end up on my back again. I've picked more splinters out of my behind than any one person should ever have occasion to, and I'm pretty sure the one that just wedged itself into my skin won't be the last of the day.

Hostility oozes out of him. I do a quick mental checklist. His name is Ronald Bellhouse. He was an accountant. His wife, Maryann, still lives in this house. Well, she did, anyway. His frequent moaning and thrashing has her so afraid that she recently jumped out a second-story window. I guess it's more accurate to say she currently lives at Baltimore General Hospital.

"Maryann needs you to stop this, Ronald. And I'm here to help."

His cruel laughter fills the room. "Help? How could you possibly help me? You're a mortal," he sneers.

"So, you know what you are, then?"

"I'm a god!"

7

Oh boy. That's not good. Usually they're broken-hearted about being dead, but this one is suffering from delusions of grandeur.

"Okay. Tell me, Ronald... I mean, 'god,' why you're staying in this attic, then. I mean, surely there's much more for you to see, and oversee, in the rest of the world, right?"

He looks me up and down. I can see his non-existent brain doing summersaults. I've clearly given him something new to think about.

"Unless you leave this attic, no one will know they should worship you. No one will know to be afraid of you, either."

He chuckles maliciously. "Maryann knows."

"Sure, but is that really enough? A god like yourself deserves praise and fear from millions, right?"

His eyes light up greedily. "Millions?"

"Yes. You can have it all, but only if you leave this house."

The last hint of hesitation falls away. He flies straight toward me, and I barely manage to hit the deck in time. Great. Another splinter.

As his spirit splits free of the attic where he'd become stuck, his form dissipates. "No!" he calls as he realizes the truth. Leaving the attic means leaving the human realm forever.

I stand up and dust myself off. I'll need to head to the bathroom with my trusty tweezers soon - which I keep on me at all times - but for now, I allow myself to smile at another job well-done. Maryann can come home.

CHAPTER TWO

My raven locks blend into the darkness as I exit the airport. It's a few minutes after midnight, and I'm dragging my shuffling feet toward my car. Ghost therapy takes me all over the globe. Sometimes, like right now, I wish it didn't.

Still, I can't help but feel some pride at the thought that Maryann has regained her home. Losing her husband was traumatic enough - even if he clearly wasn't the kind, decent man she'd always believed. There's no way I was going to break that illusion, either.

As far as Maryann knows, her husband's confused soul is now resting peacefully, and he spoke lovingly of their time together before he passed on. Being a ghost psychologist requires a dash of human counseling skills, too. After all, freeing a spirit is typically done on behalf of the living, not the dead.

I arrive at my rundown house. What? You thought being a therapist to the dead actually paid the bills? I'm lucky to eek by from month-to-month, but there's nothing else I can do with my life. Believe me, I've tried. The problem is that if I don't seek out the ghosts, they'll find me instead. It's always worse when they do, so I try to stay one step ahead.

I've barely unlocked the door and turned off my security system - a necessary precaution where I live - when I notice an oddly-shaped red envelope mixed in with the mail on the floor. Yes, my house is old enough that there's a mail slot on the front door.

I know I'm going to regret this, but I abandon my previous plan to take a quick shower and get some sleep. I know it can wait until morning. But what if it can't?

Sighing, I grab my letter opener and hear the satisfying rip of the seal splitting open. A sweet smell envelops my head, and I sneeze twice in a row. Pulling the parchment free of the envelope, I notice my knees are getting shaky. I must be more exhausted than I realized.

I stumble to the couch, avoiding the section my cat, Riley, tried to destroy, and sink into the brown cushion. Unfolding the letter, I'm struck by a jumbled mess of visions and emotions. This happens sometimes, and it means the ghost in question is begging for relief.

I scan the letter's contents as Riley jumps into my lap. His purrs begin like clockwork as I absentmindedly scratch his jet-black chin and cheeks. "Sorry, buddy. It looks like I'll be out of here again come dawn."

This is by far the most intriguing letter I've ever read, and I've received so many they've started to take over the coat closet. With my mind burning, I head up the thin staircase. I look longingly at the bathroom door before giving up on the idea of taking a shower. There will be time tomorrow. For now, I must sleep.

* * * * *

The plane lands at the Marquette International Airport. As a Michigan resident, I've been to the Upper Peninsula a few times, but this is the first time I've flown in. The seven-hour drive from Detroit felt like a liability, but now I have to pick up a rental car. I add the expense to my ongoing mental tally and wince. With any luck, this client will be able to compensate me better than the last.

I exit the rental car facility with a small, economical vehicle. It's not flashy, and it putzes down the highway, but it'll suffice. I'm headed toward downtown Munising, which I know from experience is barely big enough to count as a downtown area.

On the way, I take a few minutes to reflect on the contents of the letter that caused me to call my cat sitter for the second time this week. It's a good thing she lives down the block and doesn't charge much. Riley loves spending time with her, too, which makes it a lot easier to leave again so quickly. This seems like an odd case, but one that definitely requires some assistance. On the plus side, the ghost doesn't seem to have bad intentions. At least not yet.

I pull into the small downtown area of Munising and scour the buildings for the address that was indicated in the letter.

Spotting it, I realize I've just run into my first problem of the trip. Parallel parking? Ugh. I'm good with ghosts, but parallel parking is a skill I'm pretty sure I'll never master.

There's a lot of swearing and reversing I'm not proud of, but I finally manage to park somewhat respectably. I exit the rental car and see a blonde-haired woman in her late twenties eyeing me quizzically. Her left eyebrow cocks upward, and my face turns crimson. With my luck, this will be the letter writer. As if being around other people wasn't hard enough already.

I gracelessly extract myself from the rental car and manage to step in a puddle. Before I can get over the shock of having an unexpectedly cold and wet sock, the woman approaches me.

"Hi. Um... are you Ms. Bentley?"

My bad luck is clearly holding fast. Clearing my throat, I attempt to respond without doing anything else embarrassing.

"Yes. But please, call me Alex. And you must be Leslie?"

She nods her agreement, but I can see skepticism all over her freckled face. Not that I can blame her, but I'm pretty sure it has more to do with me than the spirit world. I wish she hadn't seen me struggle to park.

Hesitation lingers in the air for a few seconds before she turns on the small-town charm. "Thank you for coming. I really appreciate it, dear. And I've heard you're the best! Shall we?"

Friendlessness oozes from her words, but the same sentiment doesn't quite reach her brown eyes. Her words also give me pause. Who could she have heard that from? Most people who utilize my services want nothing more than a return to normality, which doesn't lend itself well to getting testimonials. And it's not like there's a Yelp category for ghost psychologists.

As we walk into the lobby, I'm surprised to see she owns a massage business. Ghosts don't tend to linger around places of this nature, especially if they didn't own the building.

"Can you tell me again what happened?" I ask. It seems repetitive, but I've learned this is the best way to get all of the details.

"Mrs. Felton was one of my regulars. A few weeks ago, she passed away on my table."

"I'm so sorry to hear that." I start to reach out for her in a comforting gesture but stop myself. Physical contact is something I'm not very comfortable with, which helps explain why I'm single. Well, that and the fact that my last relationship was beyond disastrous.

She continues without noticing my halted effort. "It was terrible. One second, I was massaging her feet, and the next..." A sob hitches in her throat. I look away to help her maintain her dignity. A loud honking announces she's blowing her nose.

"Sorry about that," she says. "So, like I was saying, she passed away on my table. They said it was a heart attack? But I don't know. If you ask me, she died from grief."

"What was she grieving?" I ask, but Leslie doesn't appear to notice.

"I understand she's been through a lot, I really do. But why did she have to die on my table? And why won't she leave me alone?" The whiny tone in her voice is unmistakable, and under different circumstances, I'd hold it against her.

"The problem," she continues, "is that she's scaring away all my customers. I barely paid my bills this month, and next month... Let's just say that if this doesn't work, I'm going to get tossed on the streets."

Great. Another client who can't pay enough to help keep *me* from being tossed on the streets. But what am I going to do? I've already come all this way. I might as well talk to her ghost.

"What does she do that's scaring people away?"

Leslie stares at me like I've lost my mind. "She cries and moans whenever I'm giving a massage, that's what! And let me tell you, that's the last thing people need when they're trying to relax. I can't exactly charge sixty dollars an hour to massage people while they listen to a ghost blubber, now can I?"

I shake my head no sympathetically. This is one of the biggest problems with ghosts who won't leave the place where they died. They fail to realize how much it hurts the living. In many cases, they terrify their own loved ones so much it brings on a mental breakdown. That may not be the case here, but the ghost clearly needs some closure.

"Okay, let's see what we've got," I say.

Her face becomes grim, but determined, as she opens the door into her massage studio. "Go on in," she says, while gesturing for me to enter the room first.

I walk through the doorframe, and it hits me like a ton of bricks. The enormity of this spirit's emotional baggage is beyond anything I've ever encountered before. Explosions sound in my mind. The essential oil diffuser on the right side of the room sprays the scent of pain everywhere. I'm pretty sure that's not a scent Leslie bought through a catalog.

Staggering, I fall to the floor with a thud. Her floor is carpeted, so there's no risk of splinters. I'm going to have a nasty bruise, though. My eyes are leaking from the intensity of this small space when it suddenly goes quiet. I rub my eyes a few times and wipe away the remnants of my tears. And that's when I see Mrs. Felton.

It's instantly clear to me she's unlike any other ghost I've ever met. There's a hopefulness in her dead eyes that makes them look almost alive. There's also a spark of recognition that's very curious. A sweet scent enters the room; it's identical to the smell of Leslie's letter. We lock eyes for a second before I speak.

"Hello. Are you Mrs. Felton?"

A soft, sad voice fills the air. "I am, dear."

"Do you know where you are?"

She titters, but not in a malicious way. "Of course. This is Leslie's massage room. I'm quite sorry for her troubles, but I can't seem to leave. And I need to find my son first. If I don't, who will?"

Confusion clouds my face. This is already the oddest spectral encounter of my career. It's also clear this deceased woman may need my counseling services more than most. I sit on the edge of Leslie's office chair.

"How about you tell me your story from the beginning, Mrs. Felton?"

CHAPTER THREE

Sitting in my ugly little hotel room eating a greasy, overpriced pizza doesn't make the words Mrs. Felton spoke go away. I've been listening to the dead speak for more than a decade, but I've never heard anything quite like this.

According to the ghost, her teenage son, Josh, disappeared last year and was never found. This would certainly be tragic enough to make her get stuck, but it's only the beginning of the story.

If she can be believed, and Leslie seemed to think she's at least mostly reliable, there have been no fewer than twelve similar disappearances within the past decade. Mrs. Felton claims none of them have been found. Disturbingly, she thinks that's at least partially because no one from the local police department will follow up on any of the cases.

Could it be true? Are there twelve missing teens who have no one but a ghost wanting to investigate their whereabouts? I've helped spirits resolve all sorts of issues, but a missing person case may be beyond my capacity. Of course, if I don't at least attempt to do this, her spirit will remain mired in the massage studio. And how will I ever sleep again knowing someone is missing and I did nothing to help bring him home? Speaking of which, the hotel bed is beckoning to me.

"What am I getting myself into this time?" I ask the bathroom mirror. It doesn't respond. The bags underneath my tired blue eyes make it clear that any further questions need to wait until the morning.

* * * * *

"Thank you for meeting me, Leslie."

She glances nervously around the local coffee shop that's draped in early morning sunlight. "Yeah, of course. But if you don't mind my asking, why are we here instead of the studio?"

"I need to gather some more information about Mrs. Felton first." I see impatience cross her features, and I prepare for her angst.

"But I thought you were going to get rid of her! How long does it take?"

"Leslie, I need you to prepare yourself for the long haul. This isn't as simple as exterminating bugs. She won't leave, she can't leave, until she's gotten closure. And this case is way more difficult than most of them. Speaking of which, what can you tell me about her son?"

A deep sigh moves her entire upper frame. "Okay, fine. Her son? He disappeared, what, eleven months ago now? Mrs. Felton acts like he's a young victim or something like that. Truth be told, though, he was a bit of a wild card. Sixteen years old and always looking to raise a little hell. She thinks the cops don't care, but it's not that. They're pretty sure he took off on his own accord, you know what I mean?"

"Is that what you believe?"

"Well, no. I mean... look, I'm not sure, all right? I know everything Mrs. Felton used to talk about while she was on my table, and it does seem strange that so many teens have up and disappeared. Of course, most kids hate living at home, right? I know I did."

My childhood wasn't exactly sweetness and roses, so I nod along wearily.

Leslie says, "You hear stuff, though. There's a lot of conspiracy theories in this town, although most people won't admit to believing in any of them during the light of day."

"Will you give me an example?"

She squirms in her seat. I can tell this is a touchy subject, so I force myself to push past my boundaries. I lie my hand gently on top of hers. "Please? This could be important."

She glances around to see if anyone is listening, then drops her voice so low I can barely make it out. "There's a rumor that the twelve teens missing from this area are part of a bigger missing persons' ring. Kids from all over the U.P. might be part of it."

"Do the rumors indicate what's happening?"

She glances from side to side again, leans in close across the table, and whispers, "Some say the government is conducting secret experiments on Isle Royale. Others think it's aliens. It could be a cult, too. And then... no, that's too crazy, even for us Yoopers."

"Believe me when I say nothing is too crazy." I hope she'll bite at my latest invitation to spill her guts. Everyone wants to tell their story, but some need more prodding than others. When it comes to gossip, almost no one can resist blabbing.

"This stays between us?"

I catch her eyes with mine and nod.

A sigh so deep it seems theatrical pushes past her cherry red lips. "Okay, but you're going to think we're all stupid hicks or something. Which we're not! Some - and not me, mind you - believe the ancient wendigos have returned to this land and they're feeding on the missing."

I consult my internal library of the paranormal and occult, but my card catalog turns up blank. "I'm sorry, what's a wendigo?"

"Oh hell, I don't know how to explain this to you. It's just an ancient Native American legend, okay? They're a myth, like werewolves and mermaids."

"I see. Do you know which theory Mrs. Felton believed?"

"A combination of them all, if you can believe that hot mess. Me? I think they're getting high and leaving town. End of story."

"Are there any big local drug pushers, then?" I ask.

Her face turns ashen. "What are you, crazy? This is the U.P. and there's nothing to do here. Of course, there's drugs everywhere! But the last thing you should do is go looking for a drug dealer. Unless you're into meth?"

I shake my head, and I can see from her agitated countenance that our conversation has hit a stopping point. "Thank you very much for your time, Leslie."

I slap a tip on the table and rise to leave. Her hand clamps onto my lower arm, and I turn back toward her in surprise.

"When will Mrs. Felton be gone?"

"As soon as she gets some closure. Don't worry, I'll be stopping by this afternoon to chat with her again. You should prepare yourself, though."

"For what?" she asks.

I shift legs and pray she'll let my arm go soon. "She might not leave until we figure out what happened to her son."

She loses her grip, and I pull away. The hopelessness and anxiety filling her eyes will haunt me all day long.

CHAPTER FOUR

I told Leslie not to discount the possibility of something strange, but honestly, I can't wrap my head around the idea of wendigos. I've spent the past hour on my smartphone learning about the mythical creatures, and the entire idea of them being real seems ludicrous.

"You thought the same thing about ghosts once," an internal voice reminds me.

I decide to answer aloud. "Yes, but that doesn't mean monsters are real. Ghosts are, at their core, human. This is something else entirely."

An alarm sounds on my phone. It's time to go for my next meeting with Mrs. Felton. I have high hopes for a more productive session and plenty of questions to ask.

It only takes five minutes to get to Leslie's studio. As she lets me in, I can see she's quickly losing her appetite for all of this. If I'm going to help Mrs. Felton - and if I have any chance of recouping some of my trip expenses - I'm going to need to speed up the timeline.

"Hello? Mrs. Felton?"

A noxious mixture of cloyingly sweet perfume and human suffering rains down on the room as she materializes. My lungs and nose scream for relief, but I know I have to push forward as if nothing is wrong.

"Hello, dear," she says.

"Mrs. Felton, is it okay if I ask you a few more questions?"

"You can ask me anything if it'll lead to my son. You are going to look for him, right?"

The combination of sadness and hopefulness makes it hard to respond in any way other than the affirmative, so I do.

"Wonderful!"

She beams at me, and I begin to realize exactly how different she is. I've never encountered another ghost who didn't seem cold, no matter how nice the person beneath had been. Despite everything she's been through, Mrs. Felton's humanity still overflows from her apparitional frame.

"Leslie filled me in a bit today..." She interrupts with an eye-roll that's seriously impressive for someone with no eyes.

"And what did she say? That he was a no-good drug addict who took off on his beloved mama? Or maybe that aliens took him? Leslie is a good massage therapist, but she's not the kindest, nor the smartest."

"She mentioned those theories, yes, among others. Some were more colorful than others. And for what it's worth, I do think she's genuinely trying to help you. Even if doing so will help herself, too."

"I see. And by colorful, you must mean... creatures that can't possibly exist and government experiments?"

I nod in agreement. She pauses to reflect on this before continuing. "I tried every trail, Alex, including the crazy ones. And they led me nowhere."

Her shoulders hitch, and I'm amazed to see she's actually crying. And I don't mean simulating the act of crying. Tears - real ones - are piling up on the carpet. It's as if her desire to solve her son's disappearance is so strong that she's physically straddling both states of being: life and death.

"Where should I start, Mrs. Felton?"

"Maybe try asking the worthless sheriff when he's going to do his job." Anger seeps into the room, and I remind myself even the nicest spirit in the world has the potential to cause great harm.

"I'll do that," I say. "Now, I think it's best if I let you have some privacy. I'll be back tomorrow." I back out of the room, keeping my eyes on her the entire way. I needn't have worried, though, as her anger dissipates almost instantly and sadness returns to fill its place.

* * * * *

I look up at the oddly-shaped, terra-cotta brick building and chuckle when I see the sign: City Hall. In a town this small, it's not surprising the police station and local government share the same building. Still, this particular structure is a throwback to at least the 1920s. I half expect to see an outdated police van drive by with an officer hanging on to the back. I hurry toward the door as a stiff, cold breeze comes off the lake.

"Can I help you?" The acerbic manner in which this question is uttered by the woman in her mid-forties sitting behind the desk suggests she would rather be anywhere else than here.

"Yes, thank you. I'd like to speak to the sheriff, please." I smile, but not too big. I have a feeling showing too many teeth would remind the desk clerk how much she hates her job.

She lifts her half-glasses up and peers at me through them. "What's this in regards to?"

The rote question comes from a script she could probably recite in her sleep. The curiosity implied within her words doesn't reflect on her face, and I know she won't stand in my way if I play this right.

"I'm writing a police procedural novel set in a small town like this. I was hoping to interview him, if he's got a minute."

The first hint of mirthfulness tickles the wrinkled corners of her mouth and she issues one dry laugh. "Oh, he's got time, all right. And enough pride to talk to you all day long. A little tip, though, between us girls? He's a glory hog, like all male cops. If you want full cooperation, you'd best tell him his name will end up in the book."

That news isn't a surprise, but her deigning to string so many words together at once? That's truly shocking.

"I'll do that, thank you. And m'am? Can I ask your name?"

"Why?" She bristles and the deep freeze seeps back in.

"It's just you've been so helpful and all, and I want to mention you by name in the acknowledgments."

Her heart melts. "Why isn't that just the nicest... I tell you what, let me get you some coffee."

She moves through the office with a flurry of activity I would have thought impossible. The next thing I know, a coffee cup is warming my hands and she's handing me a business card with her name on it. Sally Jensen.

"Thank you, Ms. Jenson!"

"Oh, call me Sally! Everyone does," she beams. "I'll let the sheriff know you're coming." With what I can only believe is an uncharacteristic movement, she winks at me as she picks up the phone.

I feel badly about lying to her; she so clearly needs someone to recognize her in even the most meager way. Maybe I'll write a book just to put her name in it.

"Sheriff Hambler will see you now." She gestures toward the left. "Take those stairs to the top, then turn right. His office is at the end of the hall. Have fun!"

As I walk up the stairs, I hear her speak into the phone receiver again. "You'll never believe it! Our small town..." If I accomplish nothing else today, at least I gave her something to smile about.

I walk into the sheriff's office, and he isn't at all what I expected. In my line of work, it's not unusual to have run-ins with local law enforcement. Experience has taught me most sheriffs in towns like this sit behind a desk all day, and this sedentary lifestyle creates a paunch in their stomach. But not this guy.

Sheriff Hambler is wiry and energetic. I don't see any sign of doughnuts, either. Looking at his thin frame, I wouldn't be surprised if none of those sugary delights has ever passed his lips.

"You must be Mrs. Bentley?" he asks.

"Yeah, um, no. I mean, it's Ms. Bentley, actually. But you can call me Alex?" The lilting tone of my voice surprises me, as does my instant recognition that the sheriff isn't wearing a wedding ring.

"Ms. Bentley? I'm delighted to make your acquaintance." He looks me up and down like a dying man choosing his last meal. My skin burns under the heat of his stare. Things have taken a turn for the unexpected, and I haven't even asked him any questions yet.

I clear my throat in a bid to stall for a few seconds so I can regain my composure. His deep brown eyes are slightly intoxicating, but there's also something predatory in them. I open my mouth, but before any words can slip out, he takes the lead. "Are you sure you wouldn't rather discuss this over dinner this evening? My name's Chad, by the way."

I stumble for words. "Um, uh, that's nice of you, sheriff. C-Chad." My words speed up as if I'm trying to win a verbal race. "M-maybe we could get started now, though? And see how things go?" I sound like a blubbering idiot. I haven't noticed another person in this way for so long that I can't quite remember how to string together a normal, coherent sentence.

He's unfazed by my nervousness. If anything, it excites him more. "All right, Ms. Bentley. Alex." He gestures toward a chair, and I sit down.

I can't believe something as inconvenient as lust has decided to rear its ugly head right now. I have several good reasons for not dating, but they all seem to have slipped my mind. His cologne wafts toward me, and I allow myself the slightest hint of a daydream. Let's just say kissing is involved.

He stares at me with expectation, and I realize I haven't said anything for at least thirty seconds. "Okay, so I'm writing a police procedural?" *Why can't I stop making everything sound like a question?* "It's set in a small town, and I thought, who better to go to than the sheriff of a small town?"

Sheriff Hambler's grin turns from intrigued to cocky. "Well, you've come to the right place." He gestures toward numerous awards, medals, and newspaper clippings that decorate his office. I peruse them for a moment, and one thing becomes clear; this is a police officer who gets results. So why hasn't he found Mrs. Felton's son?

"So, in this story, a child has been abducted. Or that's what most people think, anyway. There's a lot of crazy gossip, though."

He laughs, and says, "Yup, that sounds about right."

"I'm hoping you can walk me through the typical procedure for handling a case of this nature in a small town that doesn't have a lot of resources?" The lilt is back. Great. I hope he doesn't notice that my face is getting red again.

"Well, that depends."

"On what?"

"The age of the victim, how long ago he disappeared, and whether or not we have any viable suspects. The victim's lifestyle would also be analyzed, of course. You'd be surprised how many so-called abduction cases end with the missing person being found living a new life a few towns over."

"Wow, people really do that?" I twirl my black hair between two fingers. This is usually a disarming technique, but I'm alarmed by how natural it suddenly seems.

He leans toward me and locks my eyes with his intensity. "Oh, yes. More than half those cases aren't a crime at all. Unless it's a crime to want to reinvent yourself, that is."

Most of the questions in my head become a jumbled mess. Why now? I need to get a hold of myself before I completely blow this opportunity. I close my eyes for a second and take a deep, cleansing breath. If he notices, he doesn't point it out.

"You mentioned it being normal for there to be a lot of conspiracy theories? How do you go about determining what's worth investigating and what's not?"

"It's simple, really. Anything that involves aliens or government coverups isn't worth my time. I follow up on pretty much anything else."

I rush forward foolheartedly. "Anything else? Even if, I don't know, let's say people claim a monster was involved." I laugh to show how crazy I think this sounds. He joins me, but his eyes turn hard.

"I'd probably advise those people to stop drinking. Or to check themselves into the looney bin."

I jot a few notes down, and he eyes me suspiciously. I know I shouldn't, but I plunge forward anyway. "Say, have you ever actually dealt with something like that?"

"Ms. Bentley," he begins. *Ouch. Ms. Bentley?* "I don't know who put you up to this, but I can assure you there's no such thing as a wendigo."

I feign ignorance. "A wendi what?"

He considers my innocent tone. "What made you choose Munising? Or the U.P. at all?"

"Oh, I just love it up here, that's why! I'm from Detroit, and as a kid, we used to come up here every summer." This is a blatant lie, and I hope he's not a good enough cop to pick up on it. "I could have chosen any small town in America, but why not come back to a place with so many fond memories, you know?"

"I'm going to give you a tip, Ms. Bentley. People 'round these parts don't take too kindly to big city strangers asking a bunch of nosy questions. And speaking of which, no, there aren't any cases like those you described. Some of the town drunkards do bring up the wendigo myth whenever there's something they can't explain, but that's just damn foolishness."

I can tell he's done with me, in more ways than one. Deflated, I thank him for his time and ask for directions to the ladies' room. I walk in, notice I'm alone, and allow myself to decompress a little bit. I didn't except to get hit on today, and I certainly didn't foresee the local sheriff getting so harsh about a conspiracy theory. Maybe it's not so crazy after all?

"He's lying, you know," a deep voice shakes my eardrums and rattles the countertops. I jump a little before turning around to face the intruder.

"Dammit! I wish you guys wouldn't do that!"

The ghost chuckles. "Sorry, lady. I thought you'd want to know the truth. He's lying." An almost vulgar look enters the dead man's sockets. "He also still wants to have sex with you. And I can see why."

Flustered, I rush out of the bathroom and make my way quickly down the staircase. I send a cursory goodbye in Sally's direction and then break free of the historic building. My heart is still racing, I'm embarrassed, and I've had way too much human contact. It's definitely time to head back to the hotel room for a nap.

* * * * *

Where am I?

I've woken in a hotel room, but that's nothing new. Disorientation holds tightly to my fuzzy brain for a few more seconds before it all comes flooding back. Along with it comes the last lingering embers of embarrassment.

I'm unsure what to do next. Counseling the dead is something that usually takes one or two sessions, and I've never been asked to play detective before.

"Am I capable of doing this?" I ask the room.

"Why not?" a sepulchral voice replies.

Dammit! That's twice they've sneaked up on me in the same day. This is all very odd.

"Hello," I wave.

"Nice to meet you, Alex."

"How did you...?"

"Girlfriend, your business card is floating all over the spirit world."

"What? How is that even possible?"

"Stop asking questions and start believing, okay? That's the only way you're going to set things right."

I muse over these words while looking at the ghost before me. He's a young black man, probably in his late teens or early twenties, and his wrists have been split. Oh yeah, did I forget to mention that? The way you die has a huge impact on what you look like as a ghost.

"I'm sorry," I say while nodding toward his wrists.

"I'm not," he replies. "This town is full of nothing but rednecks, racists, and homophobes. I'm better off, honey, believe me."

This type of talk is common from ghosts who desperately cling to the idea that being dead is better. I don't try to disabuse him of this notion, no matter how tragic I think it is.

"Are you trying to tell me wendigos are real?" I can't keep the skepticism out of my voice.

"I'm telling you to open your mind, honey. But what do I know, right?"

He disappears before I can respond. I don't know what to make of his comments. I mean, monsters aren't real. Right? I shake my head vehemently. I can't believe I've wasted even a second considering such silliness.

CHAPTER FIVE

Twenty-Four Hours Later

I've spent the past twenty-four hours Skyping with my cat (don't judge me), talking to Mrs. Felton, avoiding odd looks from locals, and encountering an enormous number of ghosts. This is unlike anything I've ever dealt with before, and it's overwhelming.

To make matters even worse, none of this has gotten me anywhere. I'm pretty sure I'm falling further behind this mystery by the second. Desperate, I head back downtown.

My breath dances visibly in the air, and I shove my gloveless hands deep into my coat pockets. I had a thin knit pair of gloves when I got to Munising, but I've lost them, per usual. Darkness is creeping across the horizon, and the temperature plummets with it. Indecisive, I hesitate between going back to the hotel and entering the local bar across the street.

Screw it. This trip has taxed me beyond my limits already, and I haven't even begun to help Mrs. Felton move on. I deserve a drink. Determined, I stalk up to the heavy, dark wooden door and push it open. A little too forcefully, in fact, but I don't hit anyone. Luck is on my side for once.

A pleasant cedar aroma fills the air. The sparsely seated patrons seem disinterested in the news show that's broadcasting the latest catastrophes from around the world. With how much damage we do to ourselves and each other on a daily basis, I can't imagine why any dead spirit would willingly get stuck in the mortal realm.

The corner jukebox comes to life with a classic rock song. I hum along, nursing my amaretto sour. I'm not much of a drinker, but I also have no interest in staring at the hotel walls again. My plan is to milk this drink for as long as possible and hope no one bothers me.

"Ms. Bentley? I mean, Alex?"

My wishes are dashed. Doesn't anyone recognize a moment of inner reflection when they see it? Sighing, I look up from my drink and almost visibly recoil when Sheriff Hambler's eyes meet mine. Is he here to bark at me again?

Taking in my guarded, surprised reaction, he removes his hat and manages to adopt a slightly abashed façade. "I'm truly sorry, miss. You and I got off on the wrong foot, and that's entirely my fault. I hope you can find it in your heart to forgive me."

My instincts are skeptical, but then again, they're always skeptical of just about everything. And it would be nice to get back on the sheriff's good side. I nod noncommittally and smile with such reservation that it's as if I'm waiting to pull it back into a frown.

"May I?" He points to the empty chair next to me. Not the one across the table, mind you, but the one that's all too close to my personal space. Turning down his request will make it harder to smooth things over enough to pump him for more information, so I give my consent.

The chair squeaks as he pulls it out, and I wince. He searches my eyes for a way in, and then apparently settles on a course of action. "With Halloween being last week and all, I assumed you were trying to yank my chain with the monster talk. But how could you know how many wendigo pranks I was called about last week?"

"Seriously? Wendigo pranks?" I'm intrigued despite myself, by both the monster talk and the twinkle in his eyes. I sit back and appraise him anew. Yup, that's what I thought; he's too handsome to be anything but trouble. Even worse, he knows it.

Confidence and a hint of flirtation drip into his voice. "Yeah. Crazy school kids. But enough about that. How are you enjoying Munising? I could give you a tour, if you'd like."

"Oh, I'm sure you're much too busy for something like that."

"Honestly?" He slides his chair closer to mine, and I can smell the liquor on his breath. "I have nothing but time on my hands. All the tourists have gone home. Well, except for you, I guess. But there hasn't been much else going on lately."

I fight back the urge to ask him why the hell he isn't looking for Mrs. Felton's son, then. Instead, I find myself twirling my hair again. Emboldened, he takes my hand and says, "Come on. Let's dance."

"Oh, I really couldn't," I mumble. I'm a terrible dancer, and I hate doing things in public that are going to attract undo attention. Despite this, I somehow find myself in his embrace while swaying from side-to-side. A rock ballad from the seventies blares through the bar's sound system, and I feel dangerously close to falling, but not on the floor.

This is a terrible idea, I remind myself, but my common sense has clocked out for a break. Our bodies press closer together. His firm grip and skilled feet lead me around the dance floor. It's exhilarating, but it's so far from something I'd normally do that I'm waiting for the alarm clock to wake me from the pleasant haze of a dream.

"Can I ask you a question, Alex?"

People love to pose this query, but it's nothing more than idle chatter. My answer doesn't matter; he'll ask his question either way. Still, I give in to the social norms by saying, "Of course."

"Do you want to learn more about the wendigo legend?"

There's a finite combination of words that can be strung together into a sentence. I could have had years to hypothesize about what would come out of his mouth, but there's no way I would have guessed correctly.

"Huh?"

My confusion is evident, and he chuckles. "I gave it some thought, and it might be good for your book, right? Plus, what's the fun of going on vacation if you don't soak up some of the local culture?"

I agree, and he plunges forward. "There's a professor who is an expert on Native American folklore. That's who started the wendigo legend, you know? Anyway, he teaches at the community college in Baraga. It's a couple of hours away, but it might be worth the trip. I can put you in touch with him, if you'd like."

"Yeah, that sounds great. Thanks!" This is what comes out of my mouth, but it's doesn't match up with my innermost thoughts. The professor in question might be interesting to talk to, but he's definitely not who I want to be in touch with right now, if you know what I mean.

The sheriff pulls away as the third song of our dancing ends. "Well, I guess I'd better be getting home now. But thanks for a lovely evening. I sure do hope to see you again soon."

His face lights up with amusement at my bewildered expression. I was sure he'd try to put the moves on me, perhaps try to talk his way into my bed. I would have said no, mind you. At least, I think I would have. But it's nice to feel wanted, you know? And that's something that hasn't happened often. For good or bad, male ghosts have been the only notable men in my life for several years. Until recently, that was exactly what I thought I wanted. But now? I'm starting to think perhaps enough time has passed since things fell apart with my ex. Maybe, just maybe, it would be okay to start dating again.

* * * * *

The ghost in my room is exceptionally chatty tonight.

"Ooh! It looks like someone had a fun night. Dish it, girl!"

Protesting in a situation like this is in my nature, but I'm so giddy from the alcohol and dancing I start talking. "Oh, what the hell? It's not like you're going to tell anyone else. I met a guy tonight," I gush. "Well, that is to say I met him the other day, but I met him in a whole new way tonight."

"So, you had sex with him? Please spare me the hetero details, okay?"

We both laugh. I can tell he's only playing a stereotype because it amuses him to freak people out. His act reminds me of a character from some movie or TV show.

Sadly, this act was probably his way of dealing during life, too. I wish he'd been himself while he was still alive. Perhaps things wouldn't have ended up this way. Since I can't change that, I'm content to have someone to gossip with who won't spread my personal business around town.

"The sheriff dances like a dream," I say while mock dancing with my pillow.

He stiffens. "Wait a minute, hold up. Hold right up. The sheriff? You mean Sheriff Hambler?"

"Yes," I grin. "I thought he was a jerk at first, but he's really quite nice."

He side-eyes me. "Well, make sure he wears a condom, okay? This isn't his first rodeo with an out-of-towner, if you catch my drift."

"I'm not going to sleep with him, geeze!"

He appears to be on the verge of saying something of consequence but changes his mind in lieu of launching into a little locker room talk.

"And why ever not? He may be a man whore, but damn is he fine. The way he fills out that uniform is proof miracles exist."

Amused, I shoot a look at my uninvited roommate. Of course, he probably sees me as the one who has taken up unlawful residence in his room. We both hold ourselves together for about half a second, then we crack up with such hilarity that the front desk clerk knocks on the outside wall. Whoops.

Enjoying this natural high, I allow myself to daydream before falling asleep. Would it be so bad to have a little fling?

CHAPTER SIX

I stop at the police station on my way out of town with coffee for Sheriff Hambler and Sally. She lights up like a Christmas tree when I hand her a coffee, even though she already has one sitting on her desk.

"Is Ch... the sheriff here? I wanted to thank him, thank both of you, for all your help the other day."

"No, I'm sorry sweetie, he's out for the day." Her newfound chipper veneer fades as she continues. "That's the way of things around here. The men take off whenever they feel like it, and they leave us women to clean up their messes and keep everything running smoothly."

I have no idea how to respond, so I say something I've seen on several movies and television shows. "Isn't that the truth?"

She chortles and lightly slaps the side of my arm. "Girl, you're as bad as me. But you have to be or else they'll push you around for the rest of your life."

I sneak a peek at her left hand. As expected, there's no wedding ring. But I get the sense there used to be one and she's still quite bitter about losing her bling. I make a bit more polite, or should I say gossipy, conversation, then turn to go. I don't make it two steps before I turn back around.

"Say, Sally, can I ask you something?" My voice lowers conspiratorially, and I echo her words of the other day. "Just between us girls?"

Her eyes are riveted, and I know I have her on my side. I launch into the first of a long list of questions that would have made an inquisitor proud.

"What's the deal with Sheriff Hambler?"

It takes a second for her to connect this first question with its hidden subtext, then she flashes a slightly perverted grin. "Ohhhh. Has someone got herself a little case of blue fever? It's okay, sweetie, almost every woman in town has succumbed to that a time or two. And a few of the men, too, although that's not the sheriff's way. He's single, if that's what you mean."

"Yeah, about that. How is *he* single."

Some of the joy departs her face. "It's actually a terribly sad story. His wife died off the coast of Isle Royale. They never found her body, but after a few weeks of searching, she was declared dead."

"Oh my gosh, that *is* terrible! Wow. I had no idea. How long ago was this?"

"Let me see," she concentrates while counting on her fingers. "One, two, three. Good lord almighty how the time flies. It's been three years already."

"And it was just the two of them?"

Somberness befalls her facial features, and I brace for the worst.

"Actually... they had a son. He was fifteen when she died. The poor boy couldn't cope with the loss of his mama. He turned to drugs, or so the rumors say, before he disappeared altogether last year."

"Wait, what did you say? The sheriff's son disappeared?"

She nods sadly. "It tore the sheriff up something awful, as you can imagine."

My feet sway beneath me, and I brace myself against her desk for support. "Do you have any idea what happened?"

"As usual, there's no official story. But the sheriff believes it was drug related."

A better chance might never present itself, so I pounce. "Does stuff like that happen around here often? Teens getting caught up in drugs and going missing?"

Her hesitation is so slight most people wouldn't notice. "Alex, I've sure loved talking to you, but I just remembered I've got a report due in a few minutes. You'll excuse me, right?"

Her lack of cooperation at the most critical juncture may have left others crestfallen, but it merely confirms my suspicions. Something is very rotten in Denmark – err, Munising. Very rotten indeed. Maybe I am cut out to be a detective after all. If what I heard the other day was true, I'll soon need a new spectral business card: Alexa Bentley, Ghost Therapist and Paranormal Detective.

CHAPTER SEVEN

With Chad gone for the day, Leslie doing a few massage house calls, and Mrs. Felton unable to offer any new information, I decide the time is nigh to connect with the professor. I study the GPS on my phone, along with a paper map, and see that the trip is going to take about two hours. I'd better get going.

The U.P. is a truly beautiful place, especially near the water. The Native Americans sure got it right when they picked the name Michigan. Or, in their native Ojibwe, mishigamaa, which translates to 'large lake.' I have to crank the heat up on the rental car to keep from shivering, but I enjoy the view of the lake as I drive across M-28. The route is also flanked by the remnants of autumn's crimson red and fiery orange leaves.

I reach the town of Harvey, and it's time to head inland on US 41. This road will take me directly to Keweenaw Bay Ojibwa Community College. As the miles fly by, I munch on a few apples and listen to an old Sarah McLachlan CD I found buried in my purse. Before it seems possible, the college comes into view.

It's a lot smaller than I anticipated, but that only means it should be easier to track down Professor Williams. Happily, I don't even have to search because someone helpful approaches and offers directions. I'm surprised the student is glaringly white, and then I realize it was silly to assume everyone here would be Native American. The college has an Indian name and sits on reservation land. It also has a few history and cultural programs to die for. Perhaps if I'd taken one of them, I wouldn't have let my ignorance color my expectations about the student body.

Even with this admonishment fresh in my mind, I'm stunned again when I meet Professor Williams. He's part of the local tribe, and he's cleaner cut than anyone I've ever met.

"Ah, Ms. Bentley, correct?" he asks while shaking my hand.

"Yes, thank you so much for meeting with me!" My words are overly exuberant, most likely in an attempt to hide my surprise. I mentally chide myself; *Wow, Alex. Would you just be cool for once?* Fortunately, he doesn't seem to notice, and before I know it, we're sitting in his office.

"So, Chad Hambler tells me you want to learn about Native American folklore? I'm happy to help," he smiles. "You're not the first author to turn to me for assistance."

What? Oh, yeah. My lie about being an author gained me this meeting. Without it, I wouldn't be sitting here, and I certainly wouldn't have warm memories from last night of a certain handsome sheriff. Determined not to let my daydreams get the better of me, I refocus my full attention on the man in front of me.

He's got short, black hair and darker skin than my pasty whiteness, but not nearly as dark as I'd expected. *Strike three,* I tell myself, cringing at my shocking lack of knowledge regarding his culture. I swear he can read my mind because he says, "I know all of this may look a bit different than you'd envisioned."

"I'm sorry," I blush.

"Don't be. How can you learn about another culture if you don't experience it for yourself? We don't expect you to come here knowing everything. But we do expect you to walk in with an open heart and open mind."

"Thank you, professor."

"Please, call me Wayne."

"Wayne Williams?"

"I know, I know. I couldn't possibly sound whiter if I tried," he jokes. "Believe it or not, Smith is now one of the most common Indian surnames. Williams isn't far behind. My father was a big John Wayne fan, to answer your other question."

I'm intrigued by how easily this man understands my thoughts. His grace at my clumsy questions is endearing, and his skills as an orator make me wish I could sign up for one of his classes.

"You're very kind, Wayne. What can you tell me about the wendigo legend?

"Ah, yes. The wendigo, such a fascinating creature! Ojibwe legends teach us that wendigo should be avoided at all costs. They're foul, supernatural creatures that survive via cannibalization and dining on humans. Of course, that's a bit repetitive because many legends say humans who resort to cannibalism are the ones who become a wendigo. They're never satisfied, either. A wendigo could burst into this room and eat both of us, and it would still leave with a gnawing hunger in its stomach.

"The name wendigo – oh, and the plural form is wendigoag, not wendigos – means 'evil spirit that eats mankind.' There are many physical descriptions, and they're all equally nasty. Most say they soar above their prey at fourteen or fifteen feet tall. Fire glows in their eyes, and their fangs are longer and more vicious than a tiger's. They might have matted, light brown fur. Alternately, they could be furless with yellow, decaying skin."

I realize I'm sitting on the edge of my seat. Uncertain if he's at a true stopping point, I risk a question. "So... do you believe they're real?"

His head cocks to the side and he loses the battle with his urge to laugh. "No, of course not. But it's a great legend, right? Spooky enough for your book, I'm betting. Oh, but there is one nugget of truth to the entire thing. Wendigo psychosis is an actual medical condition. This is what happens when someone is trapped alone in the winter and unable to find enough food to survive. In the late 1800s, Swift Runner killed his entire family and ate them. The judge determined he had wendigo psychosis at the time, although that didn't stop local law enforcement from executing him for his crimes."

"That's terrible! And you really believe wendigo psychosis is real?"

"Let's just say I believe a combination of desperation and evil can cause men to do unspeakable things. Whether it's because they had wendigo psychosis or merely murderous intentions, the result was always the same."

"Where are wendigo supposed to roam?"

"Anywhere wooded, especially in the winter. But legends do point out a clear predilection for the most remote areas available. For example, Isle Royale."

"I'm sorry, did you say Isle Royale?"

"Yes," he says as confusion scrunches his face. "But remember, it's just a legend."

He relaxes, but I get tighter than ever. I have to go to that island. "How does one go to Isle Royale?"

"You shouldn't," he blurts. Then, more slowly, he explains. "First, it's the offseason, so getting there is practically impossible. It's also not safe to be there, particularly during the autumn and winter months."

"Wendigo season, I presume?" I say lightly.

His face turns graven. "No. But believe me when I say that even if the wendigo legends were true, there are worse things than wendigoag."

"I bet you're hungry after the long drive out here," he says, masterfully attempting to change the subject. Under normal circumstances, I wouldn't be pulled off topic so easily. But he's right; I'm famished.

He convinces me to go to a local diner for dinner. I know he's being nice, and probably nothing more, but I can't help but wonder if it's wrong to be excited about the company of another man. I quickly snuff out that line of thought. I'm not in a relationship with anyone, nor am I looking to be. If I want to enjoy the company of different men on back-to-back evenings, well, that's my prerogative.

Still, it's shockingly odd that I, perpetually single girl Alexa Bentley, have noticed two men during this trip. And even odder, they both appear to have noticed me, too. At least a little bit, anyway.

Wayne casually relaxes on his side of a large, comfortable booth. The dark wooden table is so high, and the seat is so deep, that I feel like a child. Wayne doesn't have that problem, though. He towers over me with a solid frame that exceeds six feet, which puts him more than half a foot taller than me.

I take the time to truly drink him in for the first time today. Chad is handsome with his sexy swagger, but Wayne doesn't need to put his sexuality on display to capture attention. When he's not talking about his passion - Native American folklore and culture - he's surprisingly understated. This puts his face on display unmarred by conversation, and let's just say I'm enjoying the chiseled view.

We eat in silence for a few minutes, and I sneak surreptitious glances until he catches my eye. His knowing smile doesn't leave me flustered like usual, which is flustering enough on its own.

Polite chit-chat ensues. He gestures frequently with his hands while talking, and I'm taken in by how strong they appear. His gentle and polite nature meshes well with his intelligence and good looks. I wonder if Chad knows what Wayne seems to instinctively understand; he doesn't have to work so hard to get a woman's attention.

Wayne is a gentleman from start to finish, so he doesn't hit on me during dinner. He doesn't need to, either. If he asked me out right now, I'd say yes with no hesitation.

Unfortunately, we've reached the end of the evening and no such question had passed through his beautiful lips. He walks me to the car, we exchange phone numbers, and he shakes my hand again.

"It was nice to meet, you. Alex. Call me if I can be of any further assistance."

"Thank you. I will. I appreciate it!"

The beating in my chest tells me I want to initiate a less formal type of physical contact, but I resist. What is going on with me? I usually don't even like physical contact with others. But I guess the fresh U.P. air really does work miracles like so many people claim.

CHAPTER EIGHT

I awake to a text message from Leslie. She asks to meet for breakfast. I'd much rather have the first meal of the day to myself, but I should check in with her since it's been a couple of days.

Picking at the cinnamon roll in front of me, I half listen to Leslie's frustrations.

"I'm at the end of my rope here, Alex. Doing house calls isn't my style, and only half my clients are going for it, anyway. I'm flat broke because of that whiny ghost. Flat. Broke."

I know she needs some type of reassurance from me that everything will be over soon – preferably yesterday – but I can't bring myself to give her false hope.

"I have a few leads I'm following up on, but I don't know what happened to her son. You live here. Can you give me something more concrete than rumors and innuendo?

Anger drapes her face as she stabs at her breakfast. "Look, I've told you everything I know. Maybe you'd have better luck if you spent your time talking to Mrs. Felton and actually investigating instead of screwing around with Sheriff Hambler."

I reel from the verbal slap as if a bucket of water was thrown in my face. Her hostility toward me seems out of proportion for the situation, but I quickly attempt to rub some emotional balm on my wounds. She's losing her livelihood, after all. And to top it off, she's expected to pay me for my troubles. I respond as calmly as possible, given the circumstances.

"Sheriff Hambler is a nice man, but there's nothing going on between us."

"Oh, please! Do you think no one saw the sexual tension between the two of you at the bar the other night? It's practically all anyone can talk about. And if you think he's a nice guy, well... you're not half as smart as I gave you credit for."

Ouch. Yet another onslaught of her piercing slings and arrows hits my pride. The faint tickle of doubt also flits across the back of my brain. Have I misjudged Chad? It's not like two conversations and a few dances turns someone into an open book. Besides, I once knew someone for years who lied and manipulated me from day one. When that relationship ended, I vowed I would never let it happen again.

When it comes to ghosts, I never feel the need to question their words or to doubt my intuition regarding their emotions. If anything, I'm more of a ghost empath than a ghost therapist. That's how I'm able to help them; I can see, smell, hear, touch, and even taste their emotions. But human emotions? Those remain a veiled mystery. Perhaps the dead let go of the very human need to hide their personal truth in a twisted web of emotional walls and deception.

Wow. That got real o'clock fast, didn't it?

"Leslie, I *do* want to help you. It's the entire reason I'm here! Helping Mrs. Felton find enough peace to move on is my primary mission, but there are so many other factors at play here... I don't mind admitting I've never dealt with a case this complex before. Ghosts don't usually ask me to pretend I'm Nancy Drew or part of the Scooby Gang, all right? For all I know, I'm looking for someone who can't be found, or who doesn't want to be. But a deal is a deal; I'll go visit Mrs. Felton again after breakfast to see if I can help her find closure with a more conventional method."

My outburst and vulnerability hit a soft spot in Leslie, and her face sags as her anger dissipates. "Shit, I'm sorry. Look, don't listen to me, okay? I'm just a naturally grumpy person who for some reason chose a line of work that forces me to put on a happy face and entertain the most woo-centric comments in history. If I'm being honest, I'm not even sure if this is what I want to do with my life anymore."

Tears infiltrate her eyes and threaten to lay siege to her face. This is an emotion I understand all too well. I wasn't always a ghost therapist, you know. It took a while for me to discover who and what I was supposed to be, and the process was always painful. Especially when a lot of time, hard work, and money had been dumped into a venture that didn't fit. I imagine Leslie's feeling a lot like that; as if her career is a sweater that once slipped on easily but has since become shrunken and torn beyond all repair.

"Ignore my comments about Sheriff Hambler, too," she continues. "I guess I'm just jealous. I've had a crush on him for years, but he's never shown any interest in me. And then you roll into town and he's all over you. It's demoralizing, you know?"

"Well, I mean, first off, no one has been all over anyone. And if he's not interested in a beautiful woman like you, then maybe something *is* wrong with him."

I don't one-hundred percent believe my own words, but they have the intended effect. Her wounded ego has been patched up. Hopefully, we can stop squabbling and I can get back to trying to finish this case. I've been here for way too long already. Which reminds me, I need to call my cat sitter and extend her services. Again. Leslie isn't the only one who's going broke due to Mrs. Felton's refusal to move on.

* * * * *

"Mrs. Felton?"

The depth of her despair smacks me between the eyes, instantly causing a headache. It's only ten in the morning, but this day already has me wanting to go back to bed.

"I'm here, dear," she wails.

Her mental state – if a ghost can have a mental state without a brain – seems to be dwindling further with each passing day. I'm frustrated at my lack of progress and how little I have to report to her. She listens patiently as I tell her about the past couple of days, but I can tell none of it gives her hope. I turn to leave, but then her words call me back.

"Don't you think it's a bit odd that Sheriff Hambler won't investigate my son's disappearance when his own son is missing, too? What if they're connected? And isn't it also strange he went out of his way to make up with you after learning you might be on to some of the more bizarre aspects of this area? He sent you to the professor to satiate your appetite, but I bet neither of them expected you to ask about actually going to Isle Royale. Why do you think that gave the professor the heebie-jeebies, anyway?"

I'm drowning under the weight of all these questions and insinuations, including the earlier batch of unpleasantness from Leslie. It sounds like they both have ill feelings toward Chad, and maybe even toward Wayne, too. I don't know what to make of this, but I do know I need some peace and quiet if I ever hope to figure it out.

"I'm going to go now, okay?"

"Of course, dear. But promise to think about what I've asked you. It might be important."

I nod my head in the least committal way possible while speed-walking out of the massage studio, through the building's main door, and to the ice-covered streets of downtown Munising.

It's November 9. No snow has fallen yet in this part of the U.P., and that's odder than the entire mystery on my plate. As I struggle on the icy sidewalk and pull my coat's thin hood over my head, I find myself wishing this freezing drizzle would turn into snowflakes. At least then I wouldn't need ice skates to make it safely to the rental car.

Dammit! This mess must be much worse than I thought because the locks are frozen shut. How did that happen so quickly? And what now? Mrs. Felton's comments swirl in my head as I resign myself to the only option that makes sense.

A short time later, I see Chad's police cruiser carefully making its way toward me. He steps out of the car and almost falls flat on his face. Sheepishness fills his features as he realizes I saw him slip.

"Hey there," he says with a mixture of embarrassment and flirtatious energy.

"Thank you for coming so quickly!"

"No problem. It's what I do," he winks at me. "Now let's see what the problem is, shall we?"

He chisels ice away from the door and attempts to stick a deicer into the lock, but it won't turn. He grunts with the physical stress of attempting to push through the invisible barricade.

"I don't understand," he says, mostly to himself. "It's almost as if..." With that, he pulls out a penlight and shines it around the keyhole. He takes his glove off, swipes a finger across the lock, and then sniffs at the residue before giving it a quick lick with the tip of his tongue.

He glances at me, puzzled. "What the heck? Listen, I have to ask you something. Do you have a habit of pouring pop out your car window?"

I look at him with incomprehension. "I'm sorry, what?"

"You know, pop. Soda. Don't Detroiters call it pop?"

"Yes, but I don't understand the question. Do people do that?"

My confused response is enough to satisfy his curiosity. "Your lock has the distinct flavor of a certain locally made red pop. Here, try it yourself." He motions toward the frozen lock, but I turn down the fortunately rare opportunity to taste it.

"What does this mean?" I ask, still flustered by the oddness of this occurrence.

"Well, I hate to say it, but it looks like someone froze your locks shut on purpose by spraying freezing cold pop directly into the cylinders. They probably used an old air compressor can or something. Or else they randomly happened to hit your car with a spray of pop without leaving a can behind. But the odds of the pop actually dripping into the lock on its own are astronomical, so I'm going with option A."

The cold moves past my skin and sinks into my bones. "Why would someone do that?"

His puzzled face echoes his spoken sentiment. "I wish I knew, Alex. But come on, let's get you out of the cold. I'll send Joel out to fix this."

"Joel?"

"Joel Haddonfield. He's the local locksmith."

My head is spinning from this seemingly unprovoked attack. Why would someone target my car locks? And how did they get away with it without getting caught? They must have moved fast because I visited Mrs. Felton for less than thirty minutes.

"Say, what brings you to this part of town, anyway?" I've been dreading this question.

"I wanted to get a massage. I met the lady who owns the studio. Leslie? She said she couldn't fit me in today as she rushed out the door. Then I decided to check out the rest of the building to look for anything else of interest."

He seems satisfied with this answer. "Yeah, Leslie can be a bit odd at times, I guess. I hear she gives a good massage, though. Come on, hop in my car."

I do as he suggests. He drives the short distance to the police station as I wrack my brains trying to figure out who might be mad at me for some reason. Then it hits me – Leslie is the most obvious suspect. I don't want to believe she'd do such a thing, but it's theoretically possible. I'll need to be more careful around her moving forward.

A welcome blast of heat threatens to melt my face off as we enter the City Hall and Police Station building. Sally's seat is vacant.

"Is Sally out to lunch?"

"Huh? Oh, no. She's on vacation. She takes two weeks off every year in November and goes down to Florida to visit family. I believe she flew out last night. Lucky, eh? She gets to enjoy some fun in the sun, and all I get is yet another postcard to add to my collection."

I'm stunned she didn't mention this the last time we spoke. Then again, it's not like we're close friends.

"Sounds lovely," I say, which is how I know most people would reply. The truth, though? Nothing against Floridians – I know a few, and they are lovely people – but every time I go there I deal with ornery ghosts, bugs the size of my head, and temperatures so hot I constantly battle sweat dripping into my cleavage. The idea of going there on vacation gets a hard pass from me. As my teenage neighbor would say, 'sorry, not sorry.'

The shock of having someone purposefully freeze my locks shut still has my mind turning summersaults. I've had enough time contemplating it to realize something else odd happened today; Chad didn't ask me where I wanted to go, he just drove me to the police station. I wish he would have taken me back to the hotel, instead.

"Want to get something to eat? There's a place a couple of doors down that will deliver to us."

I'm hungry, so it's a tempting offer. But as much as I'd like to spend some time with Munising's gorgeous sheriff, I also want to have some time alone to think.

"Actually... well, I don't mean to sound ungrateful or anything, but would it be possible for me to catch a ride back to the hotel?"

"Ah, I thought you might be wondering why we came here. The hotel's parking lot is a sheet of ice and will be for at least another hour or so. They've put up a barrier blocking entry. Besides, Joel will have your car ready by then, and it will be easier to give you a lift back to your car than to hoof it back and forth to the outskirts of town. Make sense?"

Yes, it does. So why can't I relax? I force my lips to do their best imitation of a sincere smile and then sit down. "Well, all right then, what's for lunch?"

* * * * *

Joel called Chad a few minutes ago and we're on our way to pick up my car. The entire thing took less than an hour, and spending lunch in Chad's company ended up being a nice distraction. Now I'm zoning out in a carb coma, but I'm fairly certain I can make a ten-minute drive before crashing out altogether.

With my car unlocked and the engine warming up, I hug Chad goodbye. At the last second, I give his right cheek a quick peck to show my gratitude. "Thank you again, I don't know what I would have done without you!"

His swagger returns harder than ever as he saunters back to the police cruiser, and he almost falls again. Chuckling to myself, I drive slowly to the hotel and am relieved to see the barrier is gone and the parking lot has been salted.

I stagger to my room, yawning the entire way. I can't wait to take a nice, long nap. When I swipe my electronic keycard, though, it refuses to admit me. I swipe it again several times, but the red light persists in obstinately blinking. "What the hell is wrong with all these locks today?" I say to the empty hallway.

Grumbling, I plod toward the lobby. The young, dark-haired desk clerk greets me with a warm smile. After I tell him my troubles, he assures me I don't need to worry. "This happens all the time. It's usually nothing more than interference caused by a cellphone. Did you happen to keep them together in your purse?"

"Hmmm... I don't know. It's possible."

"Well, either way, here you go! This keycard is all charged up and ready to go. Have a great afternoon, Ms. Bentley!"

His cheerfulness grates on my tired nerves – seriously, who is *that* chipper about resetting a keycard? – but the entire experience seems worth it when the happy little green light greets me and the door unlocks. Two seconds later, my hopes for a nap are dashed.

CHAPTER NINE

I shriek and the front desk clerk runs my way. "What is..." He doesn't finish his sentence. My room has been trashed. My small amount of travel provisions has been dumped all over the place, and my tiny notebook computer is smashed into several worthless pieces.

I turn on the desk clerk. "How could you let something like this happen? You had to have heard it!"

All the color drains from his face. The only thing left is the nervousness that's highlighting his features. "I'm sorry, miss. I have no idea *how* this could have happened. I've been at my post all day! Well, wait. I mean, with the exception of when I went out to the parking lot to talk to the deicing truck driver. But I was gone for only a couple of minutes, I swear!"

I know it probably isn't his fault, but I can't keep the anger out of my voice as I issue a stern command. "What are you waiting for? Call the sheriff, dammit." I fume as he slinks away. This is officially my oddest day in Munising. Is it just a series of unfortunate incidents or am I getting closer to the truth?

"I tried to stop them," the ghost says, "but they either couldn't hear me or didn't care."

Yes! I forgot about my roommate for a minute. I bet he can help me solve this particular mystery.

"Who was it?"

"I don't know. But whoever it was wore a green ski mask and bulky clothes. I don't even know if the person was male or female."

The desk clerk returns to my side. "Who are you talking to, miss?"

The ghost mockingly repeats the man's questions while waiving its illusory hands in front of the man's face, but he remains oblivious.

"What? No one," I say.

In a huff, the ghost vanishes while saying, "No one, huh? I'm out."

Great. That's yet another injured ego I'll need to soothe later. But first, someone needs to pay for this mess. I've lost some valuable things, along with any sense of privacy and security the room's lock once provided.

Chad arrives with another police officer I haven't met yet and a crime scene photographer. I'm impressed. In a town this small, I thought I'd be lucky to get one cop taking pictures with their smartphone. Turns out my preconceived notions are wrong for at least the dozenth time during this trip alone. I'll examine this tendency in myself when this is all over, I promise. For now, I rush to Chad's side.

He's courteous, but in a formal, police officer type of way. If I thought there'd be any comfort in his arms, I'm mistaken again. Crap. This is getting embarrassing. How can I keep messing up so badly?

I'm hurt, but I try to understand it's part of his job. I mean, he wouldn't exactly look professional enough to catch a criminal if he ran into each crime scene looking to hug scared female victims, right?

This calms me down. Still, I can't help but wonder if I'm placating myself to let him off the hook. A simple hand on my shoulder or the usual interest in his eyes would make me feel less alone, but he offers neither.

We go through the few details I can offer four times. Seemingly satisfied, he excuses himself to repeat the same exercise with the front desk clerk and the cleaning staff.

Meanwhile, I'm stuck trying to figure out what my next move should be. I don't feel safe here anymore, but there's nowhere else nearby that's even somewhat within my budget.

It seems like forever, but it's only been about ninety minutes since the break-in was discovered when the police finally clear the room for cleaning. One of the housekeepers helps me set things as right as possible. She eyes me sadly, and I keep getting the impression she wants to say something. No dice, though.

The temperature in the room plummets after she leaves, and the sickly metallic odor of blood swirls around my feet. This could only mean one thing; the ghost is back, and he's brought some of the anger and melancholy that led to his death with him.

Before he can finish materializing, I launch into damage control mode.

"Thank you for coming back and thank you for telling me what you saw. You know I don't think you're no one, right? I just didn't want the nosy desk clerk to cause you any problems."

"Whatever." His sullen tone is devoid of the rich flavor to which I've grown accustomed.

"Can we talk?"

He peers at me through angry, misty eyes and says nothing. Since he didn't deny me permission to speak, I'm guessing I have a chance to do what I do best. I've been so caught up in Mrs. Felton's mystery and my unusual romantic interests that I failed to see the aching need for ghost therapy in my own room. It's time to correct this error.

"I know I haven't known you for very long, but I do know you're witty and kind. You've made me laugh several times, and you tried to stop the person who smashed up my stuff. Only someone with a good heart does stuff like that."

"Aren't you forgetting something?"

"What?" I ask.

"I don't have a heart! I don't have anything anymore! And I've been stuck in this ugly, cramped hotel room for more than a year. I don't know how the hell you've stayed here so long."

I channel my attentions and energy in his direction. I don't know how or why but doing this often seems to work in a similar manner to giving an upset human a hug. At first, he tries to resist. Soon, though, he allows me to comfort him.

"You don't have to stay here anymore. I can help you leave," I offer.

He tilts his spectral head toward me with disbelief. "But isn't suicide a mortal sin? I figured that's why I was stuck here. That or maybe God really does hate gay people." His expression contains enough raw emotion and unexpressed thoughts to fill a complete set of encyclopedias.

My vision becomes blurry as tears of sorrow leak down my face. "What are you crying for?" he asks.

I ignore his indignant tone and tell him the truth. "I hate that we live in a world where people like yourself are made to feel so much pain over something you can't control."

"Newsflash, Alex. I don't *live* anywhere anymore."

This is the type of snarky outburst I've grown accustomed to throughout my career as a ghost therapist. It's not nearly as nice as the unusually kind encounters I've had with several ghosts in Munising, but its familiarity brings me some comfort. I know what to do when they're angry and spiteful. It's when they're kind and hopeful that I get tripped up or forget to do my job altogether.

"Tell me your story. I don't even know your name. We could start there."

The glass on my bedside table smashes to the ground and tosses shards everywhere. I don't think this is merely his anger, though. I think he's trying to show me how he died, so I stand patiently and quietly. He has the floor right now, and I want him to know it's okay to talk.

A dripping sound echoing in the bathroom catches my attention. I sneak a peek through the open bathroom door and discover my bathtub is overflowing with blood. A few years ago, this would have caused me to shriek and run, thereby ruining the client-therapist relationship. Instead, I continue to do and say nothing.

"Impressive," he says, but not in a nice way. I know there's about to be a whole lot more headed my way. No matter what, I must hold my ground.

The harsh squeak of a chair being dragged across a tile floor starts at a low volume, but it soon reaches a point where I'm certain my ears are bleeding. I can barely see through the torture, and it's all I can do to keep myself from retching all over the floor. As if this room needs any other unscheduled remodeling.

I brace myself against the weight of a noise that hits me like a tornado. My feet slide, but I doggedly keep my arms at my side. I'm pretty sure he won't toss me against the wall.

* * * * *

I wake up in a crumpled heap on the floor. Yup. I sure guessed wrong on that one, huh? My head is ringing from the collision, but the good news is the shrieking noise is gone. The ghost is hovering above me, and he seems at least somewhat mollified.

"I'd help you up, but, well, you know..." he says.

67

"No worries," I shake him off with the flick of my wrist. We lock eyes, and I see some contrition. I can also see it wouldn't take much for him to fly off the handle again, so I need to tread very carefully.

"I experienced something the other day that taught me a thing or two about preconceived notions. Whether they're good or bad, they're usually wrong. I'm sorry people let their preconceived notions get in the way of knowing the real you."

I can see the struggle on his face. Part of him wants to trust me, but the other part? Well... it would destroy me, if given half a chance. Like I said before, even the kindest ghosts are harder than their former selves. All I can do now is wait him out and hope he makes the right decision.

The floor trembles. I'm losing him. It's time for a Hail Mary pass.

"I've really enjoyed our talks!" It's not a lie, so saying these words in a sincere, friendly tone is easy. Will he pick up sarcasm or deceit anyway? It all depends on what channel he has his internal tuner set to. Even humans listen to everything through their own radio signal, after all.

A burst of anger shoots out of his hands and smacks the wall above me. A framed photograph of the Pictured Rocks splinters and slams to the ground, sending shrapnel flying through the room. I inhale sharply as a few choice pieces pierce my flesh. For the first time ever, I find myself wishing I had just gotten splinters instead.

He sags onto the side of the bathtub. The phantasmal blood flows freely again, but this time, it's coming from the open wounds on his arms. "I'm sorry," he murmurs with downcast eyes.

"You're full of so much pain. Please, let me help. What's your name?"

His pause turns into a long moment, but he finally relents. "Terrell."

"Terrell, I'm really glad to have made your acquaintance. Will you please tell me what happened?"

His eyes try to spark the fading embers of fury into a new, roaring fire, but they're unsuccessful. He slips backward into the bathtub.

"I was in love. His name was Dustin. S... his dad wasn't okay with it. They had a terrible fight, and he showed up at my doorstep. No one else in town knew about us, at least as far as I know. But what was an interracial, gay, teenage couple going to do? We stayed in the closet."

A flicker of surprise crosses my face and sends my eyebrows skyward.

"I was nineteen when I died. Dustin was seventeen when he came to me that day, but his eighteenth birthday was less than a week away. It's not like the age difference was weird. At least not for us, anyway."

He stops to see if I'm judging him. I'm not. "Of course not. When I was sixteen, my boyfriend was eighteen. People talked then, too," I say.

"He asked me to run away with him. I wanted to, I really did. But I couldn't. I told him we'd never get far anyway. I thought he'd calm down by the morning, so I asked him to stay over. When I woke up the next morning, he was gone. I never saw him again. No one saw him again. Or if they did, they never admitted to it."

This news is electrifying, but I'm afraid to stop him long enough to ask follow-up questions.

"When he left, it screwed me up big time. I drank. I did drugs. But none of it helped. A few weeks later, his dad paid me a visit. By the time he left, I had two black eyes and some cracked ribs. I thought that would be the end of it, but it wasn't.

"He followed me everywhere. Constantly knocking on my door, lighting up my phone, and sending me hate mail. He outed me to the entire town, too, so slurs and graffiti all over my car became regular occurrences. The last time I spoke to Dustin's dad, he told me the world would be better off if I killed myself. So, I came here, rented a room, got wasted, and did exactly what he'd suggested."

The air between us is heavy, and I notice for the first time that I'm crying. I've heard a lot of awful stories in my time as a ghost therapist, and Terrell's not my first suicide case. But this is by far the most appalling, most tragic thing I've heard to date. I wish I could wrap my arms around him to let him see he is accepted. He is worthy of respect and love. Since I can't, I focus on sending these feelings to him.

We say nothing for a few minutes. The understandably somber mood rolling off of him is lifting. "Alex... I hid my life by staying in the closet. And in death, I adopted the persona of one of my favorite TV characters. But I was never myself unless I was with Dustin. Don't make the same mistakes as me, okay?"

I nod as tears continue to stream down my hot cheeks.

"And one more thing. Be careful. This town is more dangerous than you know. Don't trust anyone."

"O-okay," I say. "I'll miss you."

He smiles and slips back into his persona one last time. "And I'll miss you, girlfriend." Casting the stereotype aside again, he locks eyes with me. "Actually, there's two more things. Be careful, and if you somehow happen upon Dustin during all of this, tell him I loved him. I never had the courage to say it when I was alive."

"I will. I promise."

I close my eyes for a few seconds and wipe my tears with my sleeve. By the time I reopen them, he's gone.

After everything I've been through today, all I want is to decompress by taking a nap, eating some greasy food, and watching television. Before I can do any of that, I have to dig the glass shards out of my skin. My trusty tweezers come to the rescue again.

With my skin newly freed of glass and some bandages slapped over the worst spots, I trudge to the front desk and report that a framed photo fell off the wall. "Maybe it was hanging loose from the intruder?" I don't know if the front desk clerk believes this, but he sends the same housekeeper back to the room. She chooses to be mute this time, and doesn't make eye contact, either. Curious.

I finally lie down on the bed. I'm drifting when a hard pounding comes from my chest. My eyes fly open, and I jump out of bed. My nerve-endings sizzle with electricity, but I can't find any reason for it. Then I realize what's tipped off my fight or flight system; the front door isn't as secure as I'd like. There aren't many options, so I improvise by pushing a desk in front of it. This might not keep someone out forever, but it should at least give me a few extra seconds to adopt a defensive stance.

With my fears somewhat allayed, my body melts into the mattress almost instantly. My grasp on the real world is tenuous at best. A tiny shred of my psyche digs its heels in with a desperate last attempt at keeping me awake, but it quickly loses the tug-of-war match.

CHAPTER TEN

My bleary eyes protest, but I push them open anyway. A beeping tone alerts me to the presence of a voicemail. It turns out, I actually have a couple of them, along with a few text messages. My pulse picks up as I scan through them, but this time, it's not because of fear. Wayne is coming to town for the evening. Based on the initial time stamp, he might be here already. Without hesitation, I call him back, internally humming at the thought of seeing him again.

"Hello?"

"Hi, Wayne? It's Alex. Um, Alexa Bentley."

"I'm glad you returned my call." His happiness is obvious from his tone, but there's an undercurrent of urgency, too. "Are you free for dinner?"

"Yes!" I say, perhaps with a little too much enthusiasm. "When?"

"How about in fifteen minutes?"

"Can we make it twenty?"

"No problem. Meet me at the café on East Munising Avenue?"

"I'll be there."

Excitement and surprise have carried me this far, but now it hits me – why is Wayne in Munising? It certainly seems like an unplanned, spur of the minute trip. Or else he didn't think of me until the last minute. I hope it's the former.

As promised, I arrive exactly twenty minutes after we hung up. He's waiting for me outside, despite the howling wind and biting cold that's still laced with the occasional burst of sleet. Recognition brightens his features, and he opens the door for me.

The delicious aroma of melting cheese, coffee, and books greets me. It's not quite what I expected, but we've got everything we need. The café's kitchen offers a nice variety of sandwiches. They also have handmade ice cream for dessert. Score! There's an attached secondary room with some tables, games, and a small selection of books for sale. Wayne leads me to the most private table in the entire establishment, and we start demolishing our dinner.

With half a grilled cheese and some chips in my system, I'm finally ready to slow down long enough to find out what's brought him to town. "So, what brings you to Munising?"

"This is the part where I'm supposed to say 'you.' And that was definitely an added incentive, but I was called down to discuss a police matter."

"What?" My eyes shoot open. Could he be involved in what happened to my room? Or even worse, is he somehow connected to the disappearances?

As if he can read my mind, he lightly touches the top of my hand and sets the record straight. "There was an animal print Chad needed help with, and I'm pretty good at that. I'm a big cliché, right?"

"Aren't we all, in one way or another?"

Appreciation replaces the sheepishness that had marred his gorgeous face. "Yes, I suppose we are," he says. "Truthfully, though, I usually try to identify prints from a photo or video. But... well, I wanted to see you. And not just because I enjoyed your company so much the other day."

A hint of darkness befalls his eyes and mouth. "I believe you're in trouble, Alex."

"Boy, you can say that again! You wouldn't believe the day I've had."

The darkness grows as I tell my story. "That's exactly what I was afraid of. I shouldn't have tried to be so coy when you asked about Isle Royale. You clearly need to know, and someone involved in that wretched place is clearly on to you."

"Wretched? Isn't it one of the most beautiful, unspoiled areas in the Midwest?"

"It used to be," he says. Anger seeps from his pores. "Now, it's not fit for anyone, especially during the off-season. See... well... small towns have a lot of secrets, and the U.P. is full of them. There's also an extensive mining system beneath Isle Royale, and if my sources are correct, it's being used for illegal purposes."

"Like what?" It's probably not wise, but I've become completely enthralled by Wayne's story. The storyteller has managed to catch quite a lot of my attention as well.

His tall frame shifts awkwardly. "I think it's drug smuggling. Could be some money laundering, too. It makes perfect sense considering how isolated the island is. People can't legally go there from November 1 through April 15, and it's not exactly a high priority for the National Park Service during that time."

The back of my mind is whirring faster than an overheated computer's fan. Wayne's words are stacking on top of each other, but I know there's more to them than meets the eye. If only I could spread them out to see how they fit into the greater puzzle that is this entire area. I'm certain if I had enough uninterrupted time, I'd be able to solve the mystery they contain. And with any luck, it would help settle the mystery of what happened to Dustin and Mrs. Felton's son, too.

"Hey," Wayne says, interrupting my train of thought. "What's fun to do here in the evening? Want to go dancing?"

* * * * *

We end up at the same bar where Chad and I pressed our bodies closely together. Years of social conditioning – plus my mother's voice – keeps telling me it's wrong to be out with another guy so soon after spending time with Chad. But why is that? I push back against this programming, making sure to focus on the fact that no one would call a guy out for dancing with two different women several days apart.

Emboldened, I'm the one who makes the first move this time. Wayne might be just as handsome – or maybe even more so – than Chad, but he doesn't intimidate me in the same way. Being around him is fun and natural. I'm definitely interested in him, but I could also see him becoming a close platonic friend.

Our dancing is looser than my last time here. I can't believe I'm on a dance floor again. Even crazier, I'm having a hoot! That can probably be at least partially attributed to our decision to stick mostly to faster songs. This isn't the type of dancing that resembles sex with clothes on. It's much more innocent, but it's just as intoxicating.

After several turns of the jukebox, we return to our seats. I'm a bit winded and sweat is trickling down my back. It seems so natural, though, like all is right with the universe. I realize I actually trust this man already. Lord help me, right?

The clock at the bar strikes midnight. When did it get so late?

"Oh, wow. It's really late, and you've got, what, a two-hour drive back? I'm sorry."

"Don't be," he smiles. Unlike Chad, his smile seems natural. It's not a tool he uses to get the attention of women. It's just Wayne being Wayne. "It's sweet of you to be concerned, but I'm not going back tonight. I'm crashing at Chad's place."

Oh no. My forehead explodes with tiny droplets of sweat. I don't know if U.P. guys are as gossipy together as what I've experienced from Sally and Leslie, but if they are, I'm sunk. What will they do when they find out I've danced with both of them?

"Who's the better dancer, by the way?" His smile has widened into a grin so big it threatens to crack his face.

"W-what?"

"Between me and Chad? Who's the better dancer? Unless you've been out dancing with someone else?" He's only gently teasing me. That much is obvious from his tone. But I was already so worried about it, I've become instantly mortified.

Seeing my panic, he reaches for my hand. "It's nothing to worry about, Alex. We're all adults, and we're all just getting to know each other. Besides, you don't live in the U.P., so we know the score. No matter how much fun we have, it's going to come to an end eventually."

His rationalism and maturity are commendable. It also sours my mood. "So, you wouldn't care if I danced with every guy in the U.P., then?"

"Do you want to dance with every guy in the U.P.?"

He can see I'm getting upset, but he doesn't RSVP to my invitation to join me in the land of irrationality. At first, this irks me. However, after a few seconds, his steadfast approach calms me way easier than expected. Chad might be a walking billboard for male sexuality, but Wayne exudes a level of peacefulness that's in rare supply. He's right, though. Nothing permanent could ever come from any of this. I might as well keep sampling both local flavors.

With that in mind, I decide to take control of the situation by avoiding any silly goodbye handshakes. Instead, we embrace, and the remnants of my previous reluctance to be involved with anyone starts melting away like a snowman on a sunny day.

What happened to me in the past is never going to happen again. I've gained too much strength and independence to let it. This conviction echoes through my mind as our lips press together with a spark. I taste beer on his breath.

Unwilling to let myself drop completely into the deep canyon of my repressed feelings, I pull away a couple of heartbeats later. I can tell I've managed to surprise him. I can also tell one kiss was enough to make Wayne question his former certainty that we're all just having fun.

CHAPTER ELEVEN

Harsh sunlight bounces off the rental car's windshield. I'm headed to breakfast with Leslie again, and I'm not sure how to handle my suspicions. I don't believe she had anything to do with the hotel room break-in, but that doesn't necessarily absolve her of guilt for the frozen car locks incident. She did have a motive – even if it's shaky, at best – and the opportunity. All it would have taken to put these two things into a ball of trouble was enough maliciousness and the know-how to pull it off.

We say hello right away, but not much else passes between us until we've put our orders in and each had a few sips of coffee. She looks at me with a hint of regret, but is it simply for speaking to me angrily yesterday? Or did she sabotage my car, thereby enabling the culprit to break into my room?

She breaks the silence first while fidgeting in her seat.

"Look, I'm sorry I was such a jerk yesterday." Her tone is far from the most conciliatory one I've ever heard, but I don't think that's due to a lack of sincerity. I get the distinct impression that giving someone an apology is harder for her than facing a nearly empty bank account at the end of each week. I understand pride, so I decide to make this process a little easier on her.

"It's really nothing. Having a ghost in your studio scaring your customers away is tough."

She nods and rips open her third sugar packet. As the white crystals mellow her coffee's bitterness, she speaks up again.

"Yeah. Thanks. I don't understand why she can't leave already, you know? I even wrote you like she suggested..."

"Wait, what?"

She doesn't seem too peeved by my interruption. It appears I've thrown her a bit off her mental track, though, and it takes a few seconds for her to get back on course.

"Before she died, I mean."

The tension in my muscles abates some, but there's still an unwelcome coil of energy inside each of them. "What do you mean?"

"She's been looking for Josh since last December. She died less than a month ago. So that was about ten months of trying anything she could think of to find him. Or to find someone else who stood a better chance of bringing him home."

Leslie stares at me like the rest of the story should be obvious, but I'm not sure I get it yet. "And... I'm sorry, that led to me how?"

"She found a column about you in a New Age magazine. It said you were like the dog whisperer of the spirit world. She figured if that was true, maybe you could tap into the ghost network and find him. Or something like that. Anyway, she never relaxed for even a second while on my table. She told me all about her different plans instead, including contacting you."

"She didn't..."

"I know. She never got the chance. We talked about that the day she, well, you know."

I can't believe it. Some random article I didn't even know existed is responsible for my being here. I'm also stunned by the deceased woman's plan to plug me into the spectral network in the hopes of rooting out her son. Does that mean she'd begun to declare him dead in her mind? Or did she truly think unconnected ghosts would possess, and freely offer, enough clues to unravel the mystery?

I resolve to ask Mrs. Felton all of these questions. First things first, though. I mentally cross Leslie off my list of suspects. With that task completed, I dig into the most flavorful waffles of my life. The secret is a whisper of cinnamon that dances on my taste buds. I've been to many towns, both big and small, but nowhere else has impressed me quite as much with its selection of breakfast food.

I promise Leslie I'll talk to Mrs. Felton today, but first, I ask for two coffees to go and make the short drive to the police station. The piping hot paper cups keep my hands from freezing in the blustery wind as it practically picks me up and pushes me through the entrance. I notice my palms are sweating as I walk up the stairs, but I don't think it's because of the coffee.

Will Chad be mad at me about last night? Will Wayne be here? Did Wayne tell Chad about our kiss? And how in the world did I get myself pulled into a love triangle?

"Why, hello." I almost drop the coffees. Chad's voice comes from behind me, and I'm so preoccupied with my anxiety I had no idea he was there. He walks around me and into view. His face is scruffier than usual. This isn't my preferred aesthetic, but on him, it looks surprisingly good.

"Did you bring me coffee again?" A gleam enters his eyes. Flustered, I hand him a coffee instead of replying verbally. "Thank you, pretty lady. Who's the other one for? Hoping to run into Wayne, too?"

He winks as the familiar crimson response steals over my face. "Don't be silly! I thought we could enjoy a nice cup of coffee together." His expression makes it clear I chose my words wisely. I congratulate myself on such a nice save.

"Come on in, then." He motions toward his office, flashes me his dazzling grin, and turns around without waiting to see if I'm going to follow. I do, of course, and we fall into our routine of chatting about mostly nothing, while he somehow infuses as much flirtatiousness into his words as possible.

A short time later, I announce my intention to leave. He crosses over to my side, gives me a hug, and whispers "it was nice to see you" in my ear. I reply in kind as I pull away, and I see disappointment flit through his eyes. Did he think he'd get a kiss just because Wayne did? Is he actually into me or is this just some type of macho thing? I don't know, but it cinches my decision not to kiss him this morning.

Frustrated by the end of our encounter, I wander into the downstairs bathroom without remembering what happened last time. Fortunately, the ghost of a man who can only be described as rough around the edges declares his presence before I get into a compromising position.

"Still messing around with the sheriff, then? You ain't got any sense, have ya?"

I ignore the insult. This is the perfect opportunity to test Mrs. Felton's theory.

"Say, do you know anything about the missing Felton boy? He's a teenager who vanished last December?"

"Maybe."

"I'd be very much obliged if you told me what you know."

A cruel smile twists his already hardened features. "And I'd be much obliged if you sucked my..."

If he had corporeal form, I'd slap him across the face. Since I don't have this option, I try something new. All the anger and hurt feelings from the past twenty-four hours are rolled up into a big ball of ugliness in my stomach. I mentally throw it in his pockmarked face.

The emotions connect with their intended target. Most ghosts simply vanish when they no longer want to be seen. He appears to shatter into thousands of pieces, but it doesn't last. Even worse, he's become more distinct, and he's wearing the most pissed off look I've ever seen.

Before he can launch a full-scale attack, I jump to the bathroom door and throw myself free of his current home. The lobby floor ripples beneath my feet as I scramble for the building's exit. The difference between making it out and ending up in a world of pain comes down to a fraction of a second. Luck is apparently on my side for once.

* * * * *

"Mrs. Felton, I hate to sound insensitive, but what's your plan if I can't find your son?"

Her sigh breaks my heart. "I know I can't stay here forever, dear. If you give it all you've got and nothing comes of it, I'll have to accept that it's my fate not to know. But how can that be true?"

"I don't know," I say, more to the ground than to Mrs. Felton. Her sorrow brings up feelings of inadequacy. I've been able to help more ghosts than not, but most of them merely needed someone to listen to their story. I'm completely out of my league here. But I can't give up and walk away from everything. At least not yet.

"I'll keep looking." My mind has been puzzling over every piece of information I've collected, and a couple of things have just snapped into place. With renewed vigor, I say, "I think I know the best place to check next."

CHAPTER TWELVE

The public library is even smaller than the one my underfunded high school had. Still, it has a collection of old newspapers and computer access, along with a charming relic: microfiche.

I tap on the keys of the lone computer. My first search brings up one news article about Josh Felton's disappearance.

I decide to try a different track. It takes a little while, but my budding sleuthing skills bring me to a piece about Chad's deceased wife. It's dated three years ago tomorrow.

Keweenaw County, Michigan – Munising resident Diane Hambler is presumed dead after an extensive three-day search. Her moored, heavily damaged boat turned up on the east side of Isle Royale three days ago. Her husband, Munising Sheriff Chad Hambler, helped coordinate the search effort. Mrs. Hambler is survived by her husband and fifteen-year-old son. A candlelight vigil is scheduled for tonight in Copper Harbor. If you have information about Diane Hambler's accident or disappearance, please contact the local sheriff's department.

There it is, in black and white, and it's still hard to believe. Chad lost his wife, followed by his son. I know how much pain can change a person, and I certainly haven't trusted anyone enough to share all of my story. But I'm still a bit confused as to why he's never mentioned his family. And oh my god, the anniversary is tomorrow, and I flirted with him this morning like a disrespectful idiot.

Someone's been breathing down my neck for a while, so I finally relent and hand over the computer station. A theory is forming in my subconscious, and it directs me to the microfiche files. Two hours later, I emerge equally sickened and victorious. There is a pattern to these disappearances, and it's not something that started recently.

I've found evidence of U.P. teenagers – along with the occasional adult – vanishing off the face of the Earth in quantities ranging from one to five per year, every year, going back at least two decades. All of them lived within three miles of Lake Superior. Their hometowns were located between the Porcupine Mountains and the Pictured Rocks. Even odder, every single missing person who fits into this pattern disappeared between early November and late March. Most of the cases center around the months of November and December, though.

The microfiche paints a disturbing picture. Aside from the vast catalog of disappearances I've uncovered – fifty-nine, to be exact – the level of reporting on each case has dwindled with each missing teen. By five years ago, most cases were given one line of text buried in the back. A few teenagers only made it into the paper when their parents paid for an ad.

What in the world is going on here?

I'm reeling from the massive scope of this ever-expanding mystery, so I ignore it when the temperature changes and the sickly scent of roses wafts toward my nostrils.

"Are you going to find them?"

Jolted, I look all around and see no one. My senses have returned, and the emotions surrounding this specter are quite strong. I make sure the door to the microfiche room is closed before I quietly open my mouth.

"I'm going to try."

"Well, that would definitely be a first," the ghost librarian says.

"What do you mean?"

"Those missing kids should be all over the national news, and the FBI should be scouring the area for them. But that's never happened, nor is it ever going to. Some superstitions go way too deeply."

"I don't understand…"

"Until you do, you won't find them."

"Can you help me? Give me something, anything, to help me figure it out."

She appears to ponder my pleading request. A lightbulb comes on in her mind. And I mean that quite literally, by the way.

A dim spectral light bulb lights up the inside of what has now become her transparent brain. This is a new trick, but I don't have time to fully appreciate it. Don't ask me how or why, but I know the clock is ticking. And much like the symbolic Doomsday Clock that's been counting down to mankind's self-imposed destruction since the late 1940s, I swear I can hear time rapidly speeding up.

"You've been on the right track all along. Follow your instincts. Listen to them, not to what anyone else says. Everyone has a part to play in this, even those of us in the spirit world. This is far bigger than you can imagine."

My face becomes slack and even paler than usual as the enormity of what I've learned sends me spiraling into the darkness. The last thing I hear before everything goes black is "hurry!"

* * * * *

Ammonia infiltrates my nostrils, and I jolt awake in a haze of coughing and retching. The world comes back into view. There's a tiny, elderly woman peering at me.

"Oh, good! It worked," she says. "I've only seen smelling salts used in the movies before. Kind of exciting to give them a whirl."

"Uhhhhh," I moan. "W-what? Sorry. I-I'll get up."

"Oh, pish posh. You need to lie back and regain your strength. I bet you have low blood sugar! Happens to me all the time. I'll be right back!"

My eyes reopen as a delightful aroma catches my attention. Could it be?

"Here you go, dear. A bite of fudge will cure what ails ya!"

She's brought me mouthwateringly delicious fudge! If anyone is in angel in disguise in this town, it's definitely the white-haired woman who is looking down at me as I eat. My moans of discomfort turn into those of appreciation for a delectable treat.

"Locally made," she says. "Better than Mackinac fudge, if you ask me. And that's a tall order!"

She chuckles as I inhale the last bite. Normally, I'd take a second to myself to look for crumbs in my teeth, but if the ghost I met a few minutes ago is right, there's no time for such vanities. I climb back into the barely cushioned seat to strategize my next move.

"Do you get low blood sugar often?"

"Huh? Oh, no. That wasn't what it was," I murmur while rifling through my notes.

"Then what? Don't tell me! You saw a ghost, right?"

My head whirls quickly around in her direction. There's a hint of a laugh on her lips, and I can't decide if she's messing with me or if she knows something.

"Everyone's seen 'ol Mabel's handiwork at one time or another, dear. I'm sure she didn't mean to give you a fright. Must be your first paranormal encounter?"

"Um, no. Far from it... Mabel, you said? Who is she?"

"Legend has it she was Munising's first librarian, although I wouldn't know for sure. I might be old, but I'm not *that* old." It's then I notice how warm the elderly woman's laugh is. She's got an inviting smile, too. She might be a good source of information.

"Speaking of ghosts... have you noticed that a lot of people go missing in this area?" I ask.

Her eyes narrow a bit, but the gregarious spark within them stays ignited. "Whatever do you mean, dear?"

"Well, for example, between local talk and the newspaper, it's clear there's at least three missing person cases from the past year involving teens from Munising."

"Three, you say? I know two boys wandered off. I haven't heard about the third."

"Do you think they could be connected?"

She clutches her hands together, extends the two pointer fingers, and rests them on her lips. "I think there's a lot of things we don't know about. And probably a few things we ignore that we shouldn't. Have I heard any proof that these things are connected, though? No. Not at all."

I can't figure out if she's telling the truth. It's time to switch tactics.

"Have you talked to Mabel?"

This catches her off guard. I can see she's struggling to decide how much to say, so I try to help her out. "I ask because I did. She certainly had some interesting things to say."

With wide eyes, she reaches out and grabs one of my hands. "You really talked to her?" she asks with wonderment dripping from each syllable.

"Yes."

"Was this the first time?"

"Do you mean with Mabel or ghosts in general?"

She shuts the door to the microfiche room to ensure our privacy. "Mabel pops up occasionally to scare people, but they all report hearing a bunch of moans. It's different for you, I take it?"

"It is, yes."

"I have so many questions! Do you think you could talk to her now? You can translate!"

My inner balloon of hope springs a leak and starts deflating. For a second, I thought I might have stumbled upon someone else who can see and talk to them like me. Many have asked me to serve as a go-between, so that's nothing new. It might be useful in this situation to have a valuable resource like two librarians on my side, though.

"I can try. Mabel? Are you still here?"

A stack of microfiche containers crashes to the floor. The living librarian flinches, but quickly recovers.

"Why are *you* still here? Go. Stop this madness while there's still time!" Mabel replies.

"There!" the elderly librarian says. "I heard the moaning, but what did she say?"

I'm torn between my lie of being an author and my need to solve this case. Then I realize I *can* tell the truth, I just don't have to admit I have any idea what it means.

"Well... she asked me why I'm still here and told me to go stop the madness while there's still time."

She scrunches her eyebrows and appears to be working on the meaning of what she sees as a puzzling statement. "Stop the madness? That's what she said? Honestly?"

A few seconds pass in silence, then the veil of puzzlement lifts from her face and comprehension shines in her eyes. She's put two and two together. Now I have to wait to see if the answer is a helpful four.

She twists uncomfortably in the chair she's just claimed. "Missing teens. Ghosts. Stop the madness. And you. Where do you fit into all this?" I don't attempt an answer as I recognize she's asking herself, not me.

We're silent for one full revolution of the second hand before she speaks again. Nervousness tinges the edges of her words, but she speaks them with confidence. "Do you know much about local legends, dear? Ever heard of the wendigo?"

I'm happy she's on the same track as me now, but I can't believe there's yet another person who is going to try to explain things away with a mythical, supernatural creature.

"I've heard of it, yes."

"My grandpa told me the wendigo are real. He said when the winter brings pain and suffering, you know wendigos are near." She clasps her hands together again and leans forward conspiratorially. "I've never seen one, mind you. I'm pretty sure they don't exist. But what if they do? Or what if their legend is being exploited to cover something up?"

Fireworks spark through the sky in my mind. This is exactly the point I've been missing by stubbornly shaking my head at something that's so seemingly ridiculous. They don't have to exist. Someone merely needs to make people believe it's possible enough that they can get away with... well, whatever it is they're doing. And I'd bet dollars to doughnuts it has something to do with those missing teens and Isle Royale.

CHAPTER THIRTEEN

As much as I had wanted to somehow go running off to Isle Royale after my visit to the library, I knew it was critical to do some self-care first, including getting a solid night's sleep. That's why I'm just now waking up to my morning seven-thirty a.m. alarm. This is my seventh day in Munising. It's also the three-year anniversary of Chad's wife being declared legally dead. I don't know if I should go try to support him nonchalantly or if it would be best to just leave him alone for the day.

What I do know is that I'm jonesing for another plate of waffles and the biggest coffee cup this city has ever seen. Leslie doesn't show up this morning, but that's fine because we didn't firm up any plans to meet again for breakfast. After settling my tab and leaving the most generous tip I can afford, I bundle up to face the continuously plummeting temperatures.

The wind makes it hard to breathe. Fallen leaves skitter around my feet, and the ominous dark clouds promise the season's first snowfall. A flurry of activity catches my attention on the far side of the parking lot, next to the public sidewalk. A woman in her forties is cursing a light pole that has apparently thwarted her efforts at hanging up a flyer. I figure she's missing a beloved pet and rush over to help out.

"Can I help you with that, ma'am?"

Her raccoon eyes and black smudged cheeks are indicative of someone who hasn't slept or cleaned their face in several days. She's definitely grieving a loss, but her aching, haunted eyes tell me instantly that the flyer in her hand is for a missing child. Willing myself to stay calm and not overwhelm her, I speak again.

"Here, let me try."

At first, her face turns borderline vicious in the same way a dog sizes up someone who might be trouble. Her features soon sag, though, and her body crumples in resignation after handing me the flyer and thumbtacks.

The pole is harder than week old biscuits, but I manage to drive the red thumbtack in place on my third attempt. Having completed my good Samaritan work for the day, I read the flyer carefully, analyzing each word for hidden clues.

MISSING – Todd Jenkins. Age: Sixteen. Last seen on November Eighth, wearing a black knit hat, black jacket, red long-sleeved thermal shirt, blue jeans, and black Converse. Reward for information that leads to his recovery.

"I'm looking for a couple of missing teens, too. Do you have any info to share that's not on the flyer?"

My words don't have the desired effect. Instead of getting more clues that could help both of us, she falls to the ground, crying and shrieking hysterically. I can't calm her down, nor can I leave her wailing on the sidewalk. After a moment's hesitation, I call Chad.

* * * * *

"There you go, Mrs. Muller," Chad says as he helps the grieving woman into the police cruiser. I step up to say a weak goodbye before he shuts the door. Her hand trembles as it reaches for the front of my jacket.

"Don't let them bury this," she hisses through another round of sobs. "When the boys go missing in this town, they never come back. God help me, they never come back." The front of her thick winter coat is covered in tears, and it's so cold some of them are already transforming into frost.

Chad shuts the back door, thanks me, and plops onto the driver's seat. As he drives away, I realize he had none of his usual swagger. It was like seeing a hollowed-out version of the sheriff. A tear escapes my left eye, and it stings me as the wind whips it from my face. It's no surprise that he's not acting like his normal self today, but I still feel helpless. How can I help someone I barely know, especially when he hasn't told me about his family yet?

* * * * *

Wayne answers the phone after the second ring. "Hello?" His voice warms my stomach and calms my mind.

"Hi, Wayne. It's me, Alex."

"Hello! It's nice to hear from you," he says, and I hear the sincerity in his voice yet again. Wayne is definitely the most stable and open of my two current romantic interests. Which is exactly why I've called him.

"I need your help with something."

"Happy to help, if I can. What's going on?"

I pause a beat before responding. Once I plunge ahead, there's no turning back from this.

"I really need to check out Isle Royale, Wayne."

"Great, come on up in April, and I'll make sure you're one of the first people to reach the island during the new tourist season."

My forefinger and thumb pinch the bridge of my nose in frustration. I'm fairly confident he's being purposefully obtuse about what I'm really saying. "That's not what I mean. This can't wait."

"Alex, no. I've told you why you can't... why you mustn't go there during the off-season. You'll get yourself killed!"

"Not if I have a skilled guide with me," I coo. I hate playing the role of a damsel in distress, and I dislike manipulating him in this way even more. But this isn't like my past. If I don't get his help, people are going to keep disappearing.

"Level with me, Alex. What's really going on here?"

"What are you doing in a couple of hours?"

"Nothing special. Why?"

"Can I come see you? I'll explain everything then, I promise."

* * * * *

"You're a what?" Wayne asks. He's baffled, that much is clear, but he also doesn't seem as ruffled by the idea as I thought he might.

"I go from place to place giving advice to ghosts. It's kind of like ghost therapy in that it helps them get closure so they can move on." In the past, I would have said these words with a sheepish tone while staring pointedly at the ground. But today is different. I'm emboldened by the depth of this mystery and by how many people seem to be involved in it.

He shifts in his seat, takes a drink of a local beer, and looks me straight in the eye. We hold each other's gaze for a moment. It's as if he's searching for something deep in my soul. Most likely, he's trying to figure out whether or not he needs to call the local mental hospital. If he tells them to pick me up, that's really going to put a damper on any future dates.

"Okay, Alex. Let's say that's true. I'm not saying it is, but I see you truly believe it. What in the world does that have to do with going to Isle Royale in November? That's crazy!"

I see his eyes flicker with the possibility that me wanting to do something he deems crazy is further proof my ghost story is nuts, too. Before I can lose him down this unwelcome line of thought, I reach my hand out and place it on top of his.

"Wayne, I know this sounds nuts. You don't think I know that? I tried to tell myself it was just insanity for the longest time. But it's really not."

"But..."

I interrupt. "This is my life. It's the only thing that's ever actually made any sense. These people... these spirits, they need help. And I just happen to be able to give it to them. Well, most of the time, anyway."

As I trail off, I see him make a mental note about my last disclosure. Dammit. That's going to be yet another uncomfortable conversation. If we get out of this one without him walking away from me forever, that is. There's no sense in lying to myself; it's going to hurt if this is the last time we ever see each other. But I had no choice. If I don't get to that island, more people are going to disappear forever. And I can't live with myself if I knowingly walk away from that. As much as I like Wayne, the risk of losing him feels insignificant compared to the mystery I'm trying to unravel.

Whether it's the look on my face, the adamant tone of my voice, or something else entirely, Wayne's countenance relaxes and he relents.

"I apologize, Alex. My parents and grandparents have told me stories that would make any skeptical person shake their head, but they believe in them with all their hearts. They raised me to believe in spirits, but I stopped a long time ago when I never found any proof they were real."

"If you want proof, I can give it to you." These words fly out of my mouth like a challenge, even though I'm not actually trying to be harsh with him. "You wouldn't believe the things I've seen in Munising alone, Wayne. And I guess that's the problem in a nutshell. It's unbelievable. But that doesn't mean it's not true."

"You make me want to believe," he says. If Chad had responded with those words, I know they would have been dripping with a not-so-hidden secondary agenda. It's different with Wayne; his words ring true, and they also have an almost childlike quality. It's like I've tapped into a part of his brain he'd forgotten about a long time ago. Now he has to decide if he's really ready to listen.

"I want you to believe me. And I want to show you the truth. But Wayne, if this is too far outside your comfort zone, we can stop talking about it right now."

His eyes light up with mischievous energy. "And how, pray tell, will you get to Isle Royale, then?"

"So, you'll go with me?"

"Let's say I'm keeping my options open. I want to hear more. Whatever you've got to say, please say it. I can handle it."

I hope so. Others have said the same thing...

Now that the fight for credibility is on the back burner, I have to figure out how to launch into this without losing him again. Unsure where to begin, I simply start speaking.

"Did you know there was a suicide in my hotel room? A teenage boy? He killed himself last fall."

Wayne's eyes immediately betray two things: he's surprised by my question and he definitely knew about my former phantasmal roommate. With a quiet, affirmative nod, he makes it clear I should keep talking.

"His name was Terrell. He was gay, but he didn't feel comfortable coming out. He had a boyfriend, Dustin, but he disappeared. Just like so many other people in this town. Dustin's father apparently blamed Terrell for it, and he hounded him so much the poor boy killed himself."

"How do you...?"

I interrupt Wayne for the second time this evening.

"He died in my room, Wayne. But he didn't leave. Well, he didn't leave until after he shared his story with me, anyway. He's gone now because that's what I do."

Wayne appears torn between believing every word I say and joking about me being a ghostbuster. I hope he chooses option A, because quite frankly, the ghostbuster joke wore out its welcome a long time ago.

"I'm sorry you found out about that, um, ugliness," he says. He looks at me searchingly, and I'm not sure what to make of it. Does he think I'm too fragile to deal with the harsh reality of a small town?

"I mean, yeah, it showcases an ugly side of humanity for sure, but it's not like it's something I've never dealt with before. I feel sorry for Terrell and Dustin, of course, and I wish people had been more accepting of them. There's no need for you to apologize, though."

"Did he tell you anything else? Like the father's name?"

"No? That didn't come up. I didn't get the sense names were the important part of the story for Terrell. He just needed to be heard."

Was that relief that briefly flitted across Wayne's face? That's odd. Or maybe not. He's probably happy he's not going to have to deal with an uncomfortable level of emotions or something. That's been typical of my experience with most guys, although I thought he was different. I guess time will tell.

"So... where do they go?" he asks.

I was so lost in the process of analyzing his micro expression that I have no idea what he just asked me, so I get him to repeat it.

"Where do they go?"

"Who? You mean the ghosts?"

"Yes," he says with a touch of laughter. His expression says it all: what the heck else could I have thought he meant?

"I don't know, actually."

"Wait, what? You said you give them advice? You counsel them? But you have no idea what following your advice does to them?"

A light crimson hue creeps into my cheeks. Despite this, I'm determined to not let him shake my confidence in the vocation that has chosen me.

"Look, they're in a lot of pain, okay? They need help putting things to rest. I don't know if that sends them to some afterlife or if it just allows them to dissipate into nothingness. What I do know is they leave a lot happier and calmer than when I first met them."

In most cases, anyway...

"Okay, okay." He holds his hands up in a gesture of surrender. "But I still don't understand what any of this has to do with Isle Royale."

"I was getting to that with Terrell. Or, more accurately, with Dustin. See, he's one of a long line of teenage boys who have disappeared from the lakeshore between Munising and the Porcupine Mountains. I looked into the area's history, Wayne, and this has been happening every year for at least two decades. Someone has to do something about it!"

"You must be a hell of a crime novelist, Alex."

"Huh?"

"You know, the police book you're writing? Your detective skills must come in handy."

Here's the moment I've been dreading. I cross and uncross my legs while nervously rubbing my palms against my jeans. "Um, yeah, okay. See, the thing about that is... well, I'm not writing a book."

His eyes grow larger, and this appears to be more about a sense of betrayal than any actual surprise. "You lied to me?"

"NO! I mean... yes, I did, about the book. But that's it. Everything else has been the God's honest truth. I swear."

"Why did you lie to me, Alex? And to Chad?"

"Do you have any idea how hard it is to stroll into a new town and tell the necessary resources you're here as a ghost therapist? If I did that, I'd be laughed out of every town before I could help anyone. Or get locked up."

His face softens as he recognizes the wisdom in my words. "Yeah, that makes sense," he says. "But there's something I still don't understand. Why did you need to know about the wendigo legend?"

This is it. Once I plunge off this diving board, there's no turning back. The water might be warm and welcoming, or it could easily turn cold, choppy, and cruel. Either way, I need to see if Wayne is someone I can really trust. No time like the present, right?

"Wayne... this isn't a normal case for me. Usually, I'm in and out in a day, two days tops. But this ghost, Mrs. Felton... did you know Mrs. Felton?"

"No."

"Okay, well, Mrs. Felton's son is one of the missing teens."

He grimaces. After everything I've told him, I find it refreshing that he's still tuned in enough to care about the suffering of others. Most people don't believe me, and those who do tend to want something from me as a result. Caring about the suffering of others is the last thing that typically crosses someone's mind after learning I can speak to ghosts.

"She won't... she can't move on until she has some resolution for his case. She's stuck in a massage therapy studio where she died of a heart attack. The owner was the first one to tell me a bit about the oddness in this area. She was also the first to mention the wendigo. Mrs. Felton isn't sure about any of that, but the rumors got me digging. Each clue I find keeps pointing in the same direction – Isle Royale. And now, there's a new missing teen. If I can help bring him home with my gift, then that's exactly what I should do."

He sighs audibly, and his entire upper body moves with the displaced air flow. I see that he's wrestling with something, and I instinctively know it's best to sit back and say nothing. He'll come to a conclusion when he's ready. With any luck, it'll be the right one.

Two minutes later, I can see the mental cylinders clicking into place. He doesn't look very happy, but he is clearly determined to move forward.

"Okay. I know there's more, and I want to hear all of it first. But okay. If you need to go to Isle Royale that badly, I'll take you."

CHAPTER FOURTEEN

It's stupid o'clock in the morning, but sleep keeps eluding me. Wayne can't meet up until the afternoon, but that doesn't mean I can't keep investigating this mystery in the meantime, right?

The alien glow of my cellphone illuminates the hotel bed. I've already scrolled through so many pages of Google search results that my pointer finger actually hurts. It also seems distinctly likely that the crick in my neck will become a permanent addition. Sighing at my textbook case of obsession, I slap the phone down on the bed.

"What is happening in this town?" I ask the newly renewed darkness. No one answers. I'm not sure whether to be happy or sad about it, but one thing is clear. If I don't get a few more hours of sleep, my investigative skills – as paltry as they are – aren't going to help anyone. Except for maybe the tow truck driver who will inevitably have to pull my crashed car out of a ditch. Since I really don't want to fall asleep behind the wheel and trash the rental car, I squeeze my eyes shut with determination.

* * * * *

The blaring of the alarm clock almost gives me a heart attack. On the plus side, I must have gotten some sleep.

I hastily shower, pull some clothes on, and pack. There's no sense in paying for a room I won't be in for several days, but I make sure to tell the front desk clerk I'll be back soon. Not that I think all the rooms are going to magically get taken while I'm gone, but it still makes me feel better.

While driving through Munising's small downtown, I ponder over some of the oddness of yesterday's meeting with Wayne. Of course, the most important thing is that he's agreed to take me to Isle Royale. But why did he look so pained when I brought up Terrell and Dustin? Making a mental note to investigate this situation more closely, I parallel park a block away from the police station. For the first time ever, it doesn't take me several tries to get it right. If nothing else, at least this particular case has helped me learn a valuable skill.

Ten minutes later, I'm walking down the frost-covered sidewalk with two piping hot cups of hot chocolate in my hands. The steam from each drink hits the air with force but immediately shrivels and dies when faced with today's ridiculously cold temperature. The digital readout above the local credit union announces that it's fifteen degrees Fahrenheit, but the redness of my wind-lashed cheeks tells a much colder story.

Fortunately, I'm inside the city hall/police station building before the wind can cause any permanent damage to my exposed skin. I pause long enough to take a deep, centering breath before boldly striding up the stairs. I know I have to play my cards exactly perfectly right or I risk upsetting Chad at the worst possible time. I don't want him to find out I know what yesterday was because that seems too weird and borderline stalkerish. At the same time, I want to be here for him.

A big grin kicks the frown from his face when he sees me, but the weariness in his eyes doesn't get the same eviction notice. I understand why he wants to put on a brave front. I've done the same thing too many times to count. I hope he'll eventually open up to me, though. Not only would it help him to talk about it but I somehow get the feeling it would help me, too.

"Hot chocolate?" he asks as one eyebrow cocks up toward the sky. "Smells delicious!"

I hand him his cup and sit down.

"I'm glad you're here, Alex."

My heartbeat increases; does he want a shoulder to lean on or has he found out what I've been up to? Would Wayne tell him everything without asking me first?

"The annual Florida postcard was delivered today. Sally must have sent it out as soon as she got there," he laughs. "Anyway, she asked me to say goodbye to you. I guess you made quite an impression on her."

Relieved, I ask to see the postcard, and he hands it over. The typical Florida scene greets me. A beach, the sun, palm trees, and the ocean are all present and accounted for. I flip it over hastily, eager to read her message.

"Ouch!" The postcard exacts its revenge on me in the form of a nasty-looking paper cut. I guess that's what I get for manhandling it.

"Are you okay?" Chad's voice is filled with concern, and I feel bad about it. I mean, he's undoubtedly plagued by the emotional strain of yesterday, and here I am making a fuss about a minor inconvenience.

"I'm fine. It's nothing," I reassure him with a smile before absentmindedly sucking the blood off my finger. He chuckles, walks across the room for a moment, and then returns with a bandage.

With the fresh scent of sanitized adhesive in the air, I finally get a chance to look at the scrawl on the postcard. *How in the world does she take phone messages for Chad? I need a handwriting expert just to decipher this mess.*

He interprets my look and laughs again. "Yeah, she's not exactly going to win any awards for penmanship, huh?"

"You said it, not me," I tease him. Refocusing, the words start to make sense. As far as I can tell, she's written a short message that's every bit as typical as the front of the postcard.

"Sheriff Hambler and Crew, Florida is as beautiful as ever. Hold down the fort while I'm gone. Be back soon. P.S. – Tell Alex I'm sorry I didn't get a chance to say goodbye in person."

That's it? Chad's eyes are boring a hole through my skull, so I look up. "She's not exactly wordy or sentimental, either, I see."

The thought of Sally being sentimental about anything apparently strikes Chad as hilarious. So much so, in fact, he instantly inhales hot chocolate down the wrong pipe and begins coughing furiously. I try to reach out to him, but he waves me off while attempting to get the coughing fit under control.

"No," he croaks. "She's definitely not sentimental." Chad risks laughing again only a few seconds after his cough has settled down. "That may just be the understatement of the year, Alex. So, tell me, what gives me the pleasure of your company and this would-be assassin masquerading as hot chocolate?"

Somehow, he manages to make the last part of this question sound sensual. I had no idea anyone could be flirtatious about hot chocolate, let alone a would-be assassin. Clearing my throat, I launch into an explanation.

"I wanted to say goodbye, Chad."

Seeing the crushed look on his face hits me like a ton of bricks, and I rush to clarify. "Oh, no. No. I don't mean goodbye as in goodbye forever or anything like that. I'm just going to explore another part of the U.P. for a few days."

Relief shines in his eyes and smile. "Where are you going? And for how long?"

His tone implies he's not overly happy with my decision to go elsewhere, but he's trying hard to keep it from me. I don't intend to let him know he's failed.

"Just down the coastline a bit to pick up some more ideas for my book, that's all. I'll be back in a few days. One week, tops." What I don't tell him could fill volumes, but there's no time to explain. Plus, I'm not so sure he'd take it nearly as well as Wayne did.

"Promise to come back?" he asks with boyish impishness.

"Definitely," I say while leaning into his offered embrace. After a second's hesitation, I give him a quick peck on the lips. It feels weird to do this before taking off with Wayne, but the idea of not giving him a goodbye kiss is also uncomfortable. I have no idea how I'm going to sort all this out. But first, I need to find out what's happening to the missing teens.

CHAPTER FIFTEEN

I'm here early, but that gives me some time to go over my plan once more. By the time Wayne shows up, I'm more resolved than ever to add 'successful sleuth' to my eclectic business card. Or rather I would, if I actually had business cards.

"Hi Alex," Wayne says in an amiable but somewhat weary tone. There are bags under his slightly bloodshot eyes. I guess I wasn't the only one who didn't get the best night's sleep.

"Are you up for this?" I inquire tenderly as my hand reaches out for his arm.

"Sure. Are you?"

There's something off about his voice. He's hiding something from me, I'm sure of it. But what can I do? I've hid stuff from people for years, including him. If there's something he's not ready to tell me, I have to respect that. And yet, that's a tall order at a time like this.

"Is there anything I can do for you, Wayne? Or anything you need to say?"

"I don't suppose you've changed your mind about Isle Royale?"

"Well, no. I haven't."

"Then it is what it is, I guess. We should get moving if we're going to get to the area before nightfall. We'll spend the night at the local motel and head out to Isle Royale in the morning."

"Thank you. I really appreciate everything you're doing, Wayne. And remember, you're not just helping me. You could be helping to provide some form of closure to dozens of families."

His face blanches as he considers my words. "That's exactly what I'm afraid of," he replies softly.

Wayne has always been more reserved and enigmatic than Chad, but I've also enjoyed his fun, carefree side. Seeing him withdraw into himself makes my heart heavy. I asked this of him. There's no one else who can help me right now, but that doesn't make it feel any less wrong.

I slip my arms around him and place my hand on the back of his neck. Stroking his hair, I bury my face into his shoulder. His body tenses in surprise before relaxing into the moment. I'm torn about what to say, or whether I should say anything at all. My mouth opens and closes multiple times without uttering a peep. Finally, I decide the best thing for both of us is to enjoy a moment of silence together before the storm. If everything I've heard, pieced together, and come to suspect is even half-true, we're in for an extremely bumpy long weekend.

* * * * *

Bright sunlight breaks through the flimsy barrier of the motel's moldy-smelling curtain. Our drive yesterday was uneventful, as was our evening. I wasn't sure what to expect when we arrived at the motel, but there were two rooms reserved. I'm pretty sure Chad would have tried to pull some type of "it's the last room, let's share it," nonsense, but that's definitely not Wayne's style. Instead, we ate dinner together and then separated with the promise of meeting at 6 a.m. for breakfast.

I glance at the clock. It's 5:48 a.m. – I overslept! There goes my hopes and dreams of a long, luxurious shower. On the plus side, the water pressure seems pretty weak in the room, so I'm fairly certain I would have been disappointed anyway.

A knock on my door comes sooner than I'd like, but I have managed to get dressed and brush my teeth. I open the door and see Wayne standing there with a slight smile. "Good morning, Alex," he says with more enthusiasm than yesterday. He still seems a bit guarded and weary, but he also looks like a man who got some much-needed sleep.

Sitting at the booth in the tiny diner adjacent to the motel, Wayne begins to detail the next phase of our journey. "I was able to rent a boat. It's not much, but it should get us to the island without any serious difficulties. I do need to warn you that it will be very cold and choppy on the water. I hope you're not prone to seasickness," he laughs.

I actually do have some minor issues with motion sickness, but I choose not to divulge that fact. "Great! About the boat, I mean, not the cold and choppiness." We both laugh. "How long will it take to get there?"

"The ferries take about three hours, but we can probably cut that down by thirty minutes or so. As long as the water doesn't get *too* choppy."

I don't even want to ask what the repercussions of that would be. He reads my countenance, though, and responds to the unspoken question. "Worst case scenario? Well, aside from having to turn back, the longest trip to the island I've ever heard of was just over four hours."

The thought of not making it to Isle Royale at all sits in my stomach like a heavy brick of greasy food. Wayne must know this because he quickly continues. "I don't anticipate any problems, Alex. At least not on the water," he mumbles.

* * * * *

It's been more than two hours, and I'm struggling to hold on to my breakfast. Wayne wasn't kidding about the ride being rough. Wave after wave breaks against the side of the boat, and I'm freezing from the constant spray. The air temperature is supposed to be hovering around fifteen degrees Fahrenheit, but I swear the wind chill is at least negative twenty.

The water isn't frozen yet because the lake is so humongous, but we have encountered a few small ice floes. As we get closer to the island, Wayne's chattiness diminishes to almost zero. His mood is clearly suffering, too. I take a moment to feel badly about the impact this is having on him, but I can't quite temper my own feelings of excitement and anxiety. I have no idea what we're about to face, but if it solves even one of these missing person cases, it'll be worth it.

CHAPTER SIXTEEN

Isle Royale is way bigger than I expected. It's been in sight for quite a while, but now that we've reached the final few minutes of the boat ride, I find myself in awe. The shoreline is very craggy, and there are ice balls accumulating in several areas. Majestic trees soar above the land, and I swear the distinctive howl of one of the island's wolf residents hangs in the air.

Suddenly, my vision is filled with white spots and my head is pounding. I reel in the seat next to Wayne as an overwhelming amount of pain, misery, fear, and anger latches onto my mind. "What the..." I say under my breath as I fall to the boat's floor. Gripping my head, I roll into a ball and try to resist the call of what must be at least dozens of ghosts.

"Alex. Alex!" Wayne shouts as he tries to get my attention. "What's wrong? Dammit! I knew this was a mistake. I'm getting us out of here!"

I push through the murky haze to counter this decision. "Don't, Wayne. Get us to the shore."

He looks at me like I've lost my mind – which is kind of what it feels like – before literally tossing his arms up in frustration.

We keep heading toward the shore, and I manage to pick myself up unto my knees. And that's when I come face-to-face with the most simultaneously horrifying and awe-inspiring sight of my entire life. The island's entire shoreline is guarded by a ring of ghosts. I can't tell if they're pleading for help or trying to scare us away, but it ultimately doesn't matter. I'm going to see this through, even if it rips my mind apart.

I glance at Wayne and see the concern on his face. There's also a flicker of something else. Is that fear? I know he can't see the ghosts or else he definitely wouldn't keep steering us toward one of the flattest areas of shore. But I get the distinct impression he can feel them, at least a little bit.

The boat slips past the ghostly border. It takes everything in me to withstand the barrage of emotions. Wayne trembles as we reach the shore. His eyes are filled with warring thoughts, and I end up with a fresh batch of guilt to compound the mess I'm currently in.

He helps me off the boat, and we both stagger onto Isle Royale with our backpacks full of camping supplies. "What *was* that?" Wayne asks me.

"Do you really want to know?"

He considers this, then his firm jaw begins broadcasting his determination. "Yes, I do. And no BS, all right? Tell me the truth."

Sighing, I honor his wishes. "Okay, no BS. The entire island is surrounded by ghosts. I can feel their emotions. That's how I do what I do. But this was on a scale I've never encountered before."

His eyes widen. "Is that why everything got so cold and dark for a few seconds? I thought we'd somehow been transported to Antarctica or something. The U.P. is known for getting cold, but I've never felt the temperature drop that much before."

I sway a little, and he reaches for me. "Yes, that's what did it," I confirm. "Cold spots. They're real, but when it's one ghost, a lot of people don't notice them."

The true magnitude of what we're doing at Isle Royale fills Wayne's eyes. "They're all dead, aren't they?" he asks me fearfully.

"I hope not," I reply weakly.

What I don't say out loud is if what I just saw is any indication, then yes, they're probably all dead. We're definitely here too late for dozens upon dozens of unfortunate souls, all of whom appear to be teenage boys. The hope that I can find the three young men in particular who brought me here has fled my mind like a candle getting snuffed out by a gust of wind.

A sharp intake of air breaks me free of my thoughts. Wayne leaves my side and goes down onto his haunches. An odd-looking set of animal tracks is on the ground before us, and he appears to be measuring them against his right hand. They're somewhat human in appearance, but longer and skinnier than any person's foot I've ever seen. There's also indentions from what are almost certainly vicious, large claws. I admit I know next to nothing about animal tracks, but this doesn't match up with anything in my limited mental database.

"Wayne?"

My voice startles him. "Huh? Oh, sorry."

"What type of animal do they belong to?"

"Honestly? I don't know. But the weirdest part is this is the exact same set of tracks I looked at in Munising the other day. And I don't mean they're from the same type of animal. They looked *exactly* like this."

"Did you know there's another young man missing from Munising? His mother was putting up flyers shortly after you came to town."

He takes a deep breath, then plunges forward with great discomfort. "Yeah. I did. Those tracks weren't just odd, Alex. There was also a lot of blood around them."

"So, you mean...?"

"It's possible that boy was killed by an animal? That's one of many theories Chad is considering, yes."

"Were the tracks anywhere else in town?"

"Now that you mention it, there was another set of similar tracks. They weren't bloody or anything, so we didn't pay much attention to them."

"Where were they, Wayne?"

Recognition transforms his face. "Oh my God. They were outside the hotel. Behind it, in fact."

"Near my room?"

"Yes."

It sounds absolutely insane, but I can't help myself from asking one further question. "Could it have... I mean, is it at all possible an animal trashed my room?"

"If it managed to get inside, somehow? Then sure, that type of damage *could* have been caused by an animal. But how the heck would it have gotten in and out without being seen?"

How the heck indeed? I silently ask myself.

* * * * *

Isle Royale is almost forty-six miles long. Combine that with a width of nine miles, and we're dealing with a land mass that would take months to fully explore. Since we don't have that kind of time, Wayne recommends heading toward one of the ancient mines.

"Hiding something illegal in the mines makes the most sense," he reasons. I don't doubt that, but I also can't stop wondering what's hidden within the thicket in the middle of the island. Even though it's practically winter and most of the trees have been stripped bare of their leaves, they're still thick enough to provide a lot of cover. There's also two information centers on the island. Believe it or not, one of them is named Windigo. Wayne has no insight to share about the National Park Service's decision to choose the alternate spelling of wendigo.

There are a few trails, and so far, we've stuck to them. The woods are beautiful and carpeted by thousands of fallen leaves. Those that haven't already decayed to the point of ugliness light up the ground with vibrant hues of red and orange. But there's also a harsh, uncompromising quality that threatens to derail our search if we veer too far off the path. And that's exactly what bothers me. Why would anyone choose to hide something in an accessible area when so much of the island is harder to walk through?

Our feet snap on twigs and rocks as we boldly continue trekking across the current trail. Just as we reach a turning point, a pack of wolves appears before us. They're as magnificent as they are terrifying. I want to flee, but Wayne stops me.

"No. Stop," he whispers. "Never run from a wolf unless you have no other choice. Follow my lead."

Wayne raises his arms above his head and starts shouting. The wolves appear cowed by this, so I join in. Out of the side of his mouth, Wayne says, "Start backing up very slowly. Do not make eye contact. Keep your arms up." He then resumes yelling at the pack.

The largest wolf howls, and it echoes off the trees. Just as I start wondering why a pack of wolves is tromping around in the middle of the day, Wayne grabs my arm. Hard.

"Shit! Alex, um, we've got a very serious problem here."

My rapidly increasing heartbeat fills my ears.

"They're coming at us from the north and the west. We've got no choice but to run for it. On my mark. One, two, three, GO!"

Before I have time to let him know I have no idea which direction I'm facing or where he wants me to run, he's tearing away from me. I quickly follow, and so do the wolves. My feet pound the forest floor and pine trees scratch my face as we leave the trail behind and rush headlong into the unknown.

The lead wolf is almost at my heels. I can feel its breath on my back, and I know I'm about to die. At the last possible second, a sickeningly painful whimpering sound erupts from behind me and I feel the impact of the wolf's body hitting the ground. There's no time to look back or to praise my savior. Instead, I unexpectedly slide down a ravine.

I'm able to slow my downward trajectory just enough to escape serious injury, but my ankle still rolls when I hit the ravine's bottom. The good news is that the wolves are nowhere to be seen. The bad news is I have no idea where I am.

"Wayne?"

A bird chirps nearby, but Wayne doesn't return my call.

CHAPTER SEVENTEEN

My cellphone is, of course, out of range. I do still have my bag full of food and other supplies. My back is sheltered by the ravine, and I've started a small fire for warmth. I heard once that the best thing you can do when you get lost in the woods is stay put. Wayne knows my general location. He's probably already working his way down the ravine right now.

* * * * *

Three hours have passed. I must admit, I'm starting to doubt my original plan. If Wayne is still anywhere nearby, I should have seen or heard him by now. Even worse, the sun is starting to dip below the horizon. What if Wayne needs *my* help? It's now or never.

I take out the chalk and red ribbon Wayne put into my bag and make trail markers as I walk. I'm also extremely grateful for the tactical flashlight he loaned me. I walk out of the ravine and find a much gentler slope that heads back up to where this entire mess started. I gnaw on my nails with indecision. Should I go back up to the right where the wolves were or hike up the left side of the hill?

I debate the pros and cons until fear wins out. The left side it is, then. The climb isn't very difficult, so I manage to get to the top before the sun completely abandons me.

Despite the desperateness of my situation, I can't help but be taken in by the brilliant light show painting the sky. The stars are unlike anything I've ever seen before, and they help light my path. Even better, green and pink hues dance across the horizon. This is my first time seeing the Northern Lights. Everything I've ever heard about them was unable to accurately convey their majesty. This is something I'll remember forever. If I make it back off this island in one piece, that is.

Wolves howl in the distance and my blood runs cold. It seems I made the right decision earlier, as they're clearly on the other side of the ravine. Still, I want to put a few more miles between myself and the beasts before I rest again.

I hope Wayne is okay.

* * * * *

The insistent chirping of birds wakes me. I must have hiked for four or five hours after sundown, but eventually, I succumbed to exhaustion and took refuge in a small cave. My body and mind are begging for a few more hours of sleep, but I need to take advantage of the sun's triumphant return. Thanks to Michigan's depressingly dark and dreary winters, there are just under ten hours until darkness falls again.

Several hours later, I almost walk into a clearing before I'm halted by the sound of someone's voice. I restrain my excitement and crouch low by a tree line. If someone else is on Isle Royale right now, they're probably up to no good.

I can't hear what's being said, but I see a tall, slender woman who I'm guessing is in her mid to late thirties. She's talking to someone I can't see, and her body language strongly suggests she's not happy.

I have to get closer. I crawl around the edge of the tree line, praying that the snakes and ticks are all hibernating. That's when life decides to slap me really hard across the face. What is Chad doing here and who is he arguing with?

"How could you do this, Diane?" he shouts.

Diane? As in Diane Hambler, his dead wife?

"You're such a fool, Chad. Always have been, always will be."

I can feel his ego ripping in half from thirty feet away.

"He's our son, dammit! How could you involve him in this?"

"You have no room to be righteous. You turned him away when he needed you the most. This is your fault."

Chad says something so quietly that I can't make it out. What I can easily discern, though, is that he's deflated.

Diane says, "He came to me willingly, Chad. I didn't come for him. He asked to be part of this so he could get away from you."

With a cruel and haughty expression, she twists the emotional knife further. "You disgust me."

His face crumples, but he manages to defiantly reply. "I can't clean this up for you anymore."

"You don't need to. We'll clean it up. We'll clean *you* up."

A long, strange whistle bursts forth from her lips. There's a disturbance in the tree line directly across from me. As its maker moves into the clearing, a living nightmare comes to life. The wendigo is here, and it's running directly at Chad.

Time ceases to exist. I leave the safety of my hiding spot in an awkward, unsuccessful attempt to save him. I don't know what he did wrong, and I don't care. I just don't want to see him get ripped to shreds. The wendigo slams to the ground mere seconds before that can happen.

Sitting astride the beast is Wayne, who keeps pummeling it with his heavy binoculars. It tries to buck him off, but he holds fast. With one last, horrific crunch, the wendigo goes silent.

Wayne barely has half a second to catch his breath before Diane picks up a gun and starts shooting at him. He's halfway through the clearing and somehow manages to end up right next to me in what I swear was only three lunging steps.

He grabs my hand and pulls me with him deeper into the forest. Five minutes later, we stop, and I can see his body shaking with adrenaline. "Are you okay?" I ask.

"That was a wendigo. They're real. And I just beat one. How in the world did I do that?"

I hug him and then try to get his attention back on the bigger issue at hand: Chad is in danger, and it sounds like the missing teens might really be on the island. Or, at the very least, Diane is a very likely suspect for their disappearance.

We take a beat to discuss our plan, then quickly put it into action. It's tricky, but I believe in Wayne. That's why I'm willingly walking straight back into Diane's camp.

* * * * *

Where the heck is everyone? I thought I'd be instantly spotted and might have to dodge an incoming bullet – or a wendigo – but I don't see anyone at all. There's no sign of Chad, either, although there is a bit of blood where he was standing.

I look around quizzically. I was supposed to distract Diane long enough for Wayne to get the jump on her. I start to walk back toward the tree line when a horrible sound stops me in my tracks. The moaning and wailing that's reverberating out of the ground below me is unquestionably human.

Certain that Wayne still has eyes on me and that Chad is being tortured – or fed to a wendigo – my eyes dart everywhere. *Ah ha! There it is!* I stride toward a partially hidden set of wooden doors that are on the ground. They creak as I pull them open and dust flies into my face. The meager illumination of my flashlight shows a crumbling set of stairs leading down into the darkness.

I'm coming, Chad.

CHAPTER EIGHTEEN

The painful cries continue as I rush through the narrow corridor. A few torches hanging on the makeshift walls light my way, and I impulsively decide to grab one. Wielding nothing more than a tiny tactical flashlight and a torch, I approach the slightly ajar door that separates me from whatever atrocities are being committed here.

I sneak to the edge of the doorframe and carefully peer into the room. Chad *is* there, and he's tied to a large x-frame. His screams escape through a filthy rag and drips of blood continue to join their brethren in several puddles by his feet. Diane is his torturer, but from what I can tell, she isn't even bothering to ask him any questions.

Unsure what else to do, I creep up behind her and swing the torch as hard as possible at the back of her head. Diane crumples to the ground as her hair ignites. Freaked out, I grab a tarp and put out the flames.

Next, I remove Chad's gag and start working on untying him "Alex? What are you doing here?"

"Saving your ass, apparently," I quip.

His bewildered expression makes it clear he doesn't take in my attempt at humor. With no time to explain myself further, I begin pulling him toward the door.

"Come on, we have to get out of here!"

We make it about twenty feet down the corridor before Chad stops. "No, I can't do this. I can't leave him here."

Oh, yeah. Diane did say something about his son being here. Anxiety has chewed a hole through my belly and sunk into my knees, but I nod my agreement anyway and follow him back through the corridor. *What am I getting myself into now? And where the heck is Wayne?*

We continue to scurry through what has become an ever-expanding network of tunnels. We have no idea which way to turn, but Chad plunges headlong carelessly. Either he's following some type of police intuition or this isn't his first time in this old mine shaft. I try really hard not to dwell on the latter possibility.

A young man darts into view. He's probably fifteen or sixteen, has sandy brown hair and blue eyes. His ribs protrude grotesquely from his emaciated frame. He drops to the ground and trembles noticeably. A thin trail of urine escapes the right leg of his tattered pants.

"Please..." he croaks.

I drop to my knees. "Shhh. It's okay. You're okay. We're not going to hurt you."

His trembling increases and I wonder what type of mental torture would make him frightened of a few kind words. I reach out to comfort him, but his body jerks backward as if to avoid a venomous snake.

"Okay, I'm sorry. I'm really not going to hurt you. I'm here to help."

His furtive eyes connect with mine, and I can tell he's scanning them for any hint of deception. "What's your name?" I ask.

Tears stream from the corners of his eyes. "My name? I don't have a name here. None of us do."

I want to kill Diane and anyone else who is involved in this mess, even though that might end up including Chad.

"What was your name before you came here?"

He struggles for a moment, but then his eyes clear. "Todd. My name is Todd."

The latest missing teenager! If it wouldn't have been wildly inappropriate, I might have just broken out into a victory dance. He's not dead! I actually found him, and I've solved at least part of the mystery. I could get used to this.

"I'm going to take you home, Todd. But first, I need your help. Are there others here? Others like you? I want to take all of your home."

A sob hitches in his throat. "They're all dead," he whispers. "I'm the last."

Chad falls to the ground with a hard thud. "No. No! That can't be true. Where's my son? *Where* is he?"

Todd backs up a few inches and then begins rocking, but he doesn't respond.

"I don't believe she'd kill her own son, Alex. I *have* to keep looking for him."

"Yes, of course. Wayne should be here any second, if he's not already. Let's help Todd get out of this nightmare and then we'll find your son."

The hint of fresh air and daylight brings a spark into Todd's eyes. He pulls himself up and heads toward the exit.

"Todd?" I call after him.

He doesn't respond. I'm torn between two choices. Do I help Chad or complete a major part of my mission? I'll never forgive myself if anything happens to either of them. I'm guessing Chad is in better shape to defend himself, despite the recent torture, so I reluctantly follow Todd after Chad nods his approval.

We make our way outside without a hitch, but there are two things weighing heavily on my mind. Why haven't I seen Wayne yet? And why did the tarp that was covering Diane's body appear to be completely flat on the ground when we rushed past that room?

I help Todd find a hiding place past the tree line, point him in the general direction of our boat, and tell him to hang tight. Leaving him seems very wrong, but so does abandoning Chad. It's time to head back into the tunnels.

* * * * *

"Alex," someone thinly hisses.

No one appears in my vision, but the voice is very familiar.

"Wayne?"

"Over here," he says.

I'm overjoyed that he's finally here. That feeling stops as soon I actually see him, though.

"Oh, Wayne," I whisper sadly as I take his hand and push the hair from his forehead. The sickly metallic scent of blood hangs in the air. The tunnel wall holds his weight, but it's taking everything in him not to slide to the ground. His life is seeping from a gaping wound on his right lower abdomen.

My vision suddenly diminishes with the blurry haze of tears. "What happened?" I cry.

"She got the jump on me..."

"Diane did this?" I ask incredulously. "I don't understand, Wayne."

"Two of the... boys are h-here. T-Todd and... t-the other o-one... save them. G-go."

"No! I won't leave you here like this, Wayne. I can't!"

"Y-you must... or... all in v-vain."

I channel as much inner strength as possible, kiss him, and nod. "If we'd had more time, if we'd been in a different place... I think I would have fallen in love with you, Wayne. Thank you." I kiss him again.

As the light fades out of his eyes, he says, "H-hey... At l-least I-I'll see you... a-again." A faint smile reshapes his facial features as he exhales his last breath.

I want to fall apart. I *need* to fall apart. But Diane could be anywhere and Chad is still down here, too. Plus, there's two victims to rescue. I kiss his cheek one more time and then remove the boat keys from his inner jacket pocket.

"I'll come back for you," I pledge.

I really hope Chad is still alive.

CHAPTER NINETEEN

Grabbing another torch from the wall, I work my way deeper into the mining tunnels. Water drips from the crudely fashioned ceiling and the mustiness reminds me of a closet filled with mothballs. Odd sounds keep hitting my ears from all directions, and I'm poised for a fight each time I turn another corner.

Where is he?

This place would be disorienting enough even if I wasn't terrified. I'm pretty sure I've even managed to walk in circles a couple times, although there really aren't any discernible landmarks to verify my theory. There's nothing but a series of dimly lit, damp, pungent tunnels. None of them have led to any additional rooms or any clues about Chad's location.

Wayne's death hangs impenetrably over my heart and mind. Rationally, I know this entire mess is Diane Hambler's fault, but that's not enough to prevent me from feeling one-hundred percent responsible for what happened to Wayne. After all, if I hadn't cajoled him into coming here, he'd still be alive.

Pushing back tears, I plod forward with no clear end game in sight. Just as I'm starting to wonder if I should go back toward the surface, I hear the faint trickle of voices far ahead. My feet disobey my mental command to be cautious as they pick up speed. One of those voices is Chad's, and it sounds like he's in trouble, yet again.

I skid to a stop before bursting into view. Peering around what must be the millionth corner of this old mine, I see Chad, Diane, and a teenage boy. The young man is every bit as emaciated as Todd, and he has the rabid appearance of a dog that's been bitten repeatedly by an infected animal.

"Son, please. Put that down," Chad says. The strain in his voice is unmistakable. That's when I realize the teen who must be his son is holding what can only be described as a ceremonial knife from well before the Middle Ages. If I don't miss my guess, it's actually an athame. It's not at all shocking to see evidence of magic rituals being performed here, although I've never seen anything to suggest that magic is real.

"You threw me away like garbage! Why shouldn't I kill you? Do you understand the power in a son sacrificing his father? It would fuel us for years!"

"You're wrong. I *never* intended to make you feel like garbage. You're my son. I know I didn't react well, but I needed a little time," Chad implores him.

"Oh, don't worry, Dad. You'll have plenty of time to think while we bleed you dry." The scorn and hurt in his son's voice slaps Chad in the face and rebounds to me. His son is clearly ready to exact vengeance for any and all perceived slights, and he doesn't seem to have any interest in confirming anything first. *Judge, jury, and executioner.*

Chad hangs his head with resignation. He slowly walks toward his son, clasps his hands together, and thrusts his arms out with supplication. "Please. I never meant to hurt you."

I'm stunned by how different Chad seems. Long gone are his swagger, flirtatious energy, and seemingly endless supply of bravado. I understand what he's going through is enough to temporarily punt these qualities away from anyone's personality, but that doesn't make it any easier to see him give up so easily.

Diane pushes Chad from behind and his son roughly ties his hands together. As they lead him down the next tunnel, a faint glint catches my attention. Chad's gun! He must have dropped it or stashed it as a backup plan. If he's got that level of foresight, then he may not be as far gone as I'd feared.

With the gun firmly in my grasp, I follow them for several minutes until they reach their destination. *Great. Another x-frame. What is it with these people and their x-frames?*

The teenage boy works on tying Chad to the wooden frame as his mother watches. With everyone distracted, I'm able to position myself behind Diane. She slightly turns as I cock the pistol, jam it into her ribs, and put her into a semi-chokehold.

"Stop!" I command.

Chad's son looks at me with bewilderment for a beat before ugliness transforms his face. "What are you doing? Let my mother go!"

"Calm down. No one needs to get hurt here. Just untie your dad, and we'll all walk away from this."

"Don't listen to her," Diane hisses.

The teenager's face is filled with conflict. He sags slightly, and although he doesn't remove Chad's bounds, he doesn't continue with them, either.

"Put the athame on the ground," I say.

His startled expression tells me all I need to know; it *is* an athame, and he's shocked that I know that.

"I don't know if blood magic is real or not, but I promise you, killing your dad isn't going to give you want you want. You need to let him go."

"You need to be *strong* and do what *I* tell you," Diane contradicts me. "This silly, lovestruck cow isn't important. *I'll* deal with her. You *must* prepare the sacrifice."

"But she'll shoot you."

"Oh, I don't think that will be a problem," says a new voice. Much like Diane before me, I'm unable to turn around fast enough to see my new attacker. But as she coldcocks me, I realize I've heard her voice before.

* * * * *

Crap. These people must have gotten a bulk discount. That's the only way to explain their predilection for x-frames. I'm tied to one, and Chad is affixed to another one in front of me. His face is swollen from a fresh round of beatings he must have taken while I was passed out.

"So, you've finally decided to join us, huh?" a voice dripping with derision greets me.

As the grogginess clears from my eyes, I get definitive confirmation of what I already suspected. Sally is part of this, and she's not on the side of law and order.

"Aren't you supposed to be in Florida?" I ask.

She mockingly repeats my question and then spits out a response, "Florida is hot, muggy, and full of bugs. How in the world does anyone believe *I* would be into *that*? You're all even dumber than I thought."

Sally and I may have a shared disdain for humidity and bugs, but that's where our similarities end. I knew she was nasty. I just didn't know she was *this* nasty.

"Is this the part where you tell us all about your evil plan?" I ask as Chad watches everything carefully.

"What do you think we are? Idiots?" says Diane. "Or perhaps you think we're mustache twirling cartoon characters?"

Chad manages to whisper "moose and squirrel" just loudly enough for me to hear it, and he gives me the faintest hint of his killer smile. Not a smart idea, but it's still an impressive amount of clapback from someone who has been beaten up and taken hostage for the second time today. And it proves yet again that his psyche is less damaged by this experience than outward appearances suggest. At least so far, anyway.

"I want to tell them," Sally whines.

The two women share a brief face off before Diane relents. "Fine. Whatever. But don't take too long."

"You see, Sheriff Screw-Up and Nosy Novelist, you're about to become the guests of honor at a ceremony that dates back thousands of years. You do know how wendigos are made, right?"

What was it Wayne said? Something about... oh my god. They can't seriously mean cannibalism, right?

Sally sees my horrified moment of recognition and laughs. "Exactly," she winks before blowing out the sole torch lighting the area around the x-frames.

CHAPTER TWENTY

There's a gun that's getting so intimately acquainted with my ribs that it should probably buy me breakfast. There's no chance for me to run and nothing I can do for Chad. There's rope biting into my wrists, and I can't see anything through the itchy burlap sack that's covering my face.

Whoever has set me and the gun up on the worst blind date of all time has zero patience for the fact that I'm walking blind. My latest stumble results in my body being jerked back up as the gun probes even more insistently. I'm pretty sure it will rip through my skin and touch my actual ribcage if she presses any deeper. I'm also certain she doesn't care.

A sharp rush of coldness and the unmistakable pine scent announces we've left the mine. I hope Todd doesn't get brought back into this mess. Unless he can save us, of course.

I count my paces but lose track after number two-hundred. Shortly thereafter, I'm slammed against something wooden. *Let me guess. An x-frame?*

Yes, ladies and gentlemen, it is indeed another x-frame and someone's roughly tying me to it. If I get out of this alive, I don't ever want to see another piece of rope again. I'm also going to throw away my x-frame bookcase.

The burlap sack is ripped from my face. Stars twinkle overhead as the full moon lights up the entire clearing. An ancient drum sits nearby. It appears to be Native American in origin. Chad's son picks up a pair of large, mallet-styled drum sticks. Wildlife scatters loudly through the trees as the mallets induce the drum to sing its eerie, powerful song.

My lips tremble, but it's more from the cold than fear. That's what makes it so astounding when the teenage boy tosses away his jacket and rips off his shirt.

"It's my turn," he says manically as his mother urges him onward.

"Yes. Do it, son. Do it!" The zeal in her eyes is unmistakable. Diane is glowing at the thought of her estranged husband's death, but it's also much more than that. I'm pretty sure she actually believes in blood magic.

The athame's blade reflects a moonbeam as it plunges toward its intended target. "Please, Dustin. Stop this. There's still time," Chad says as sobs catch in his throat.

Dustin? Did he just call him Dustin?

Dustin rakes the blade down Chad's exposed chest. Blood bubbles to the surface, and Dustin uses it to paint his chest and face. "Why wouldn't I kill you, Dad? You killed the love of my life!" he screams.

"I did what?" Chad retorts.

"Stop it. Just stop it. Mom told me everything. How you killed him and staged it to look like a suicide. I hate you. I'm glad you'll be my sacrifice."

"No! That's not what happened!" I shout.

Broken from his reverie, Dustin looks at me as if he had been completely unaware of my existence until now. "What the hell would you know about it?" he screams.

"She's telling the truth, Chad. I *didn't* kill him. But I did receive a letter claiming he was responsible for *your* disappearance. Your mother wrote me; she said you came to her after he broke your heart. After he told *you* to kill yourself. I was enraged. I *never* wanted to hurt you. I was trying to protect you!"

Dustin hesitates, and I know this is my best chance. "Dustin! He loved you. Terrell *loved* you. Don't do this."

The teen's eyes shoot daggers through me. "How could you possibly know that? And who the hell are you? Why are you defending this creep? Oh, wait, let me guess. He's sleeping with you, right? Probably told you that you're special? Well, you're not."

"No, I'm *not* sleeping with him. And I know because Terrell told me himself!"

"How is that even possible?" he asks me skeptically, but I can tell I've caught his attention.

"Because I can talk to ghosts, Dustin."

Everyone holds completely still for two heart beats, then Dustin, Diane, and Sally erupt with laughter. Meanwhile, Chad gives me the most quizzical look I've ever encountered.

"I know it sounds crazy, Dustin. But it's true, and I can prove it!"

"How? How can you prove it?"

"He told me you wanted him to leave town with you, but he said no because he didn't think that would solve anything. The two of you spent the night together. You left before morning. It broke his heart, Dustin. He waited for you, prayed he'd see you again. But you never came back."

Dustin's face contorts with grief. "He's really dead, isn't he?" Tears stream down his face, and he loses his grip on the athame.

"Don't listen to this nonsense," Diane screams.

Dustin stands there, torn between what's in front of him and what he wants to believe.

"No. Ghosts aren't real," he whispers.

"I'm afraid you're wrong about that. Chad, hold on!"

While we were vying for our lives, the island's spectral residents had come to watch the action. Now, they give every indication they want to help. "I hope this works," I say to myself.

Bundling up all the fear and anger from the past twenty-four hours isn't difficult. Will sending it flying toward the ghosts affect them the same way as the creep who resides in the police station bathroom? With no time to give it any further thought, I push with everything I've got. The air ripples. It knocks everyone to the ground, except for those of us who are tied to one of these damn x-frames.

The ghosts break into a million shards before reforming. It's like putting on a pair of 3D glasses and watching them come to life on a massive IMAX screen. Chad's mouth hangs agape. I follow the direction of his gaze, and it becomes apparent he can see the ghosts. Everyone can. Startled, Diane drops Chad's gun.

Dustin clearly isn't sure whether this is really happening or he's losing his mind, but he picks the athame back up and cuts me and Chad free. "Go," Dustin says, while pointing toward the woods.

"Not without you," Chad says. Each word is infused with a mixture of awe, terror, and swagger. *He's going to be all right.*

Chad turns toward Diane and Sally. They're both too terrified to run, which is at least partially thanks to Wayne's spectral form standing a few inches in front of them. My heart wrenches at the sight of him. "I told you I'd see you again, Alex. And for the record, I could have fallen in love with you, too. In fact, I think I already did."

Obviously confused – and somehow appearing a bit jealous, even with everything that's going on around him – Chad strides boldly to the two women and picks up his handgun while declaring, "You're under arrest."

I toss him some of the rope, and he binds their hands and feet together. "How are you going to explain your roll in this, Chad? If you haul us in, you'll go to jail, too." Diane says.

Chad picks up his handgun from the ground. "Maybe that's for the best," he sighs. "This ends now. No matter what."

Before we can discuss our next move, a wendigo crawls into the clearing. Chad tries to take the athame from Dustin to protect us, but his son calls him off. "Stop, Dad. You don't understand."

The battered form of the wendigo manages to crawl to Dustin's feet before collapsing. This is clearly the same beast Wayne battled with. I can't believe it's alive, and I also can't understand why Dustin doesn't want to finish it off.

"It's all been a lie, hasn't it, Mom?"

Diane refuses to respond to her son's accusations, but Sally snorts. "Of course, it's a lie, you idiot!"

With his eyes clear for what must be the first time in months, Dustin draws close to the injured beast. Before anyone can try to stop him, the teen drops to the ground and gently strokes the creature's matted, brown, blood-soaked fur.

"It's going to be okay," Dustin says quietly. Chad tries to intervene again, but his son holds up both hands and asks him to back off.

"Here goes nothing." Dustin's hands work slowly and methodically at first. My vision is partially obscured by Chad, but I see pieces of the creature tossed to the side. *Is he dismantling it?*

"Oh, my god," Chad says in a thin voice.

"Help me sit him up, Dad."

As they prop up what remains of the wendigo's body, two things become clear. First, the wendigo isn't dead. And second? It's not a wendigo, after all. Instead, it's a confused, broken looking young man who was covered in the wendigo's skin and fur.

"What's your name, son?" Chad asks.

The former wendigo's eyes are dull and possess no hint of recognition.

"He doesn't know right now, Dad. But I do. This is Josh. Josh Felton."

CHAPTER TWENTY-ONE

The distinctive crunching of fallen, desiccated leaves interrupts a lot of stunned, random questions about Josh and how he got to the island. All of us spin in the direction of the noise, including our two prisoners. *Please don't be another wolf.*

Chad hands the athame back to his son and arms himself with his police-issued handgun. They strike a defensive pose and we all collectively hold our breath.

Voices drift into the clearing and I tense up even more. How can we know if this is good or bad news? I glance at Diane and Sally, but they seem every bit as surprised as the rest of us.

Suddenly, Todd bursts through the tree line, and he's brought the cavalry with him. A group of seven police officers and two park rangers step forward and bark at Chad and Dustin to put their weapons down. They instantly comply, and then Chad says, "I'm Sheriff Chad Hambler from Munising. Boy am I glad to see you guys!"

The newly introduced tension melts as the officers confirm Chad's identity. He quickly explains the situation and three of the men split from the group to escort us to the boats.

"How, Todd?" I ask. My curiosity about how he pulled this off when the boat keys are still in my pocket is almost as big as my gratitude.

"The boat's ship-to-shore radio, of course," he grins. It's clear he's been damaged by his time spent on the island, but unlike the others, he was here for a relatively short period of time. The joy of escaping and becoming a hero to his saviors has brought new life into his face and eyes. I can't help but wonder how he lost so much weight in such a short period of time, but I figure that's a question for another day.

We've been walking for a few hours when we approach the area where the wolves attacked me and Wayne. I stiffen out of fear, but then something unexpected fills my path. There are two wolves lying dead on the ground.

"Looks like these boys got into a fight over food and ended up killing each other," one of the park rangers says sadly while shaking his head. I don't tell him I was the food in question. Also, there goes my theory that another beast – perhaps even a real wendigo – was responsible for saving my life.

"Thank you," I whisper to the fallen canine who hurled itself at my initial attacker. A shudder runs down my spine as I realize that either of them would have eaten me alive if given the chance. I'm so glad we're going to be leaving this island soon.

* * * * *

Being processed through the local police department is a time-consuming, tedious process. Not that I'm complaining, mind you. Well, not much, anyway. After everything that's happened, I want to sleep for twenty-four hours and then have some time to myself to mourn Wayne.

All of this must be clear on my face because Chad puts on a brave, exaggerated swagger as he approaches. "Hey, pretty lady. Can I give you a ride home?" The familiar flirtatiousness has tinged his words. This is wholly inappropriate at a time like this and it should probably tick me off. But it makes me chuckle instead.

"Yes," I smile.

"You're free to go," one of the officers says. "But don't leave the Upper Peninsula without checking in with us first, okay?"

My heart sinks at the realization that I could be stuck here for who knows how long. I want to go home, pet my cat, and stop hemorrhaging money. "You're a key witness," the officer explains as he signs me out of the station.

* * * * *

At least an hour has passed with nothing more than the soundtrack of snores emanating from Dustin, Todd, and Josh. Chad's large SUV deftly cuts through freshly-fallen snow. I'm glad he didn't bring his police cruiser.

"Did you love him?" Chad asks.

I'm stunned. Not just by the question but by the timing of it.

"Honestly? Yeah. I think so."

Deafening silence fills the space between us while I count to five. Before I can say anything else, Chad says, "He was one of the best people I've ever met. You two would have been really good together."

The raw humbleness in his voice is a nice replacement for his almost constant sensuality. It also might have been enough to make me seriously consider him again if there weren't still so many unanswered questions. For example, what in the world did Diane mean when she said he'd go to jail, too?

CHAPTER TWENTY-TWO

"Hi, Mrs. Felton! I've brought Josh home!"

The ghost's presence is almost overwhelming to me, but Josh can't see or hear her. To help them say goodbye, I decide to give her a little jolt of my energy.

The rims of his eyes fill with tears. This is most assuredly a bittersweet moment for the teenager. Yes, he's finally free, and yes, he gets to talk to his mom. But this will be their last conversation ever.

Before I walk out of the room, Mrs. Felton says, "Thank you, dear! You did it! I never had any doubts. I'm forever grateful."

"Happy to help," I say as I walk out of the room, knowing that was our last conversation, too. By the time Josh exits the room less than half-an-hour later, Mrs. Felton has left the massage studio. I send Leslie a text with the good news as Chad takes me back to the hotel.

My car is in the hotel parking lot as the Copper Harbor police had promised, so at least I'll be able to wander the town if I want to. First, though, it's time to sleep. Until June.

* * * * *

Is it June already?

My cellphone loudly announces that someone wants to talk to me. Sighing at the interruption, I accept the call and hear Chad's voice on the other end.

"They're going to have us both testify, Alex. So, I guess you have to stick around for a little while longer."

"But..."

"I got the district attorney's office to agree to pay for your hotel room, car rental, and food expenses since you're a lead witness. Does that help?"

My attitude promptly improves before it even had a chance to make its worst impulses known.

"Oh, and one more thing. I got them to agree to backdate the payments all the way to your first day here since that's when you started investigating the mystery. You can drop the novelist ruse, by the way," he teases me.

"Consider it dropped," I happily reply.

"On another topic... um, look. We should probably talk. I'm sure you have a lot of questions."

* * * * *

"So, wait a minute... those mines were first used six-thousand years ago? And they were abandoned under mysterious circumstances that were later connected to the wendigo legend?"

"Exactly," Chad says.

"But what does that have to do with any of this?"

He takes a deep breath and then launches into a long explanation.

"The indigenous people were the first to mine the island. They truly believed in the wendigo legend, so when their brethren started disappearing during the winter, they decided that miners were being killed off by the beasts.

"After they stopped coming to Isle Royale, everything seemed okay. For about a year, anyway. Then the winters turned harsher than ever. Their villages were struck by disease and famine. Eventually, some of them got to talking about how mild and prosperous the previous few winters had been. And somehow, they came to the conclusion that the wendigo required a sacrifice.

"This went on for centuries. One teenage boy was taken to Isle Royale and offered as tribute to the wendigo each winter. As you can probably imagine, this didn't go over very well with the earliest European settlers. Over time, the practice stopped. Until tuberculous and a bad drought hit the U.P. at the same time.

"Desperate for answers, some of the men in Copper Harbor pleaded with the Native Americans for help. That was when the story of the wendigo was reintroduced. Thinking it was just crazy enough to possibly be true, a young man was forcibly taken to Isle Royale and sacrificed."

He pauses, and I pick my jaw up off of the ground. I can't wrap my brain around the idea that anyone ever believed there was a link between the wendigo and misfortune, let alone that they thought the answer was to sacrifice teenagers.

"Chad?"

"Yeah?"

"How does all of this connect to what just happened? And, more importantly, how does it connect to you?"

CHAPTER TWENTY-THREE

Three Weeks Later

I've never seen the wheels of justice move so quickly. I suppose that's one of the perks of small town living. The backstory Chad told me has just been repeated in the small, crowded courtroom. Murmurs ripple through the crowd, but none of them sound surprised.

"What happened next, Mr. Hambler?" the middle-aged district attorney with salt and pepper hair asks.

Chad is obviously uncomfortable in his dark blue suit. His hands persistently fidget with a red tie that's slightly too short. "From what I understand, the ritual sacrifices only persisted until the Italian Hall Disaster in 1913. After that, people lost their taste for sacrifice, and it also became increasingly more difficult to head to Isle Royale unnoticed."

"How did Mrs. Hambler and Ms. Jenson get involved in all of this, then?"

"They come from a long line of miners. And, apparently, ritualized sacrifice was also part of the family."

"Are you saying that Ms. Jenson and Mrs. Hambler are related?"

"Yes. They're cousins."

A collective gasp escapes from a few of the jury members. It seems so staged that I double-check to make sure I'm actually sitting on a hard, wooden bench in the Munising courtroom instead of watching a legal melodrama on TV.

"And why did they return to Isle Royale? What motivated the murders?"

"Objection, your honor!" barks the defense attorney as veins pop out on his thick neck. He reminds me of a dog, but not in a friendly way; more like a fighting dog that enjoys ripping others apart.

"Sustained. Counselor, let me remind you that speculation doesn't help anyone."

"I have no further questions for Mr. Hambler at this time, your honor."

* * * * *

Diane takes the stand. She's cold as ice, of course, and they don't get much out of her. I didn't expect them to, either. The most noteworthy thing about her testimony is a fresh batch of accusations against Chad. The judge shuts this down, though, and orders the jury to disregard it because Diane and Sally are the only ones on trial right now. Additionally, the district attorney seems to be concerned that allowing Diane to keep casting aspersions on Chad will make her more sympathetic to the jury.

Sally's temper and disdain for everyone is clearly going to be their undoing, though. The district attorney presses her repeatedly, and I sit spellbound by the entire spectacle.

"Of course, we used the wendigo legend to our advantage. It was a drug operation, you idiots!"

Sally's eyes open wide as she realizes her mistake. The defense attorney does a literal face palm. One thing is now written all over his bulldog face: *I'm going to lose this case.*

Diane's countenance turns murderous. Luckily for Sally, Diane's hands are currently cuffed together.

Meanwhile, the district attorney smiles. The police found evidence of drug smuggling in the mine, but until just now, the two women had vociferously denied being connected to it. That's another set of charges that's most likely going to stick.

"Why bring the kids into it?"

With a look of resignation, Sally sinks herself in deeper.

"Someone had to make, package, and transport the drugs, right?"

"There's something I don't understand," the district attorney begins.

"How shocking," Sally interrupts. They've got her cornered, and her sharp, jagged, nasty claws have come out. I'm not surprised.

Ignoring her, he says, "Why did you make the boys believe they were actually able to turn into a wendigo?"

"Look, that was Diane's thing. Something about it being symbolically perfect. She brainwashed those boys. Got them to forget their names. Got them to want to become a wendigo. Or to be sacrificed to one. Those idiots actually fought over who would become the next wendigo. Can you imagine?"

"But why? Why go that far?"

"Because she hated her life? Because she craves chaos? Because she loved keeping those boys under her thumb and wanted the drug money to start a new life? Hell, she might have even started believing in her own nonsense by the end. Take your pick. I don't really know."

Trying a new tactic, the district attorney asks, "How did the so-called wendigo tracks end up in Munising?"

"That was a stroke of brilliance, huh?" Her eyes light up as she warms to her storytelling role. "We needed another worker. And we needed to stir up the wendigo rumor to scare people away. So, we took one of the sets of costume feet and made indentions with them into the mud. Diane trashed *her* hotel room for fun and to distract the police," she says while pointing at me.

"How long have you two been doing this?"

"Oh, about twenty years now."

A hush falls over the courtroom.

The district attorney says, "Twenty years?"

"That's what I said, isn't it? Do you have wax in your ears?"

Someone in the audience tries to cover their laughter with a cough. As far as I can tell, it doesn't fool anyone.

"Why?" the attorney asks.

"It's the family business. Why not?"

Are orange jumpsuits also the family uniform? I ponder. *Because there is nothing flattering about them.*

"How did you get away often enough to make it work?"

"At first, our shifts were only for two weeks each per season. But three years ago, Diane decided to go full-time. It was a stroke of luck when she legitimately crashed her boat. All she had to do was lie low for a while until everyone believed she was dead, including her husband.

"That's when the wendigo thing started. I guess she wanted to make sure the superstitious fools in this town would never find her. Of course, she ruined that herself by reaching out to her son and her husband last year."

The two women resume glaring at each other. This time, Sally's eyes fill with murderous intent.

"How did she reconnect with her son?"

"Chad was treating Dustin like shit for being gay. I told her about it, and she asked me to bring him to her. He wasn't too keen on leaving his boyfriend behind, but Diane gave me explicit instructions. Only Dustin could come."

I feel Dustin stiffen next to me. He still blames his mom and dad for what happened to Terrell, and rightfully so. But he's also taken on a lot of guilt for his decision to leave town without Terrell by his side.

"You said this started twenty years ago," the district attorney says thoughtfully. "If my math is correct, wasn't Mrs. Hambler only eighteen then?"

"Yup, just turned. And she was quite the looker, too. Made it nice and easy to convince the first few rounds of workers to go to the island willingly. The wendigo nonsense started several years later. And I knew it was going to screw everything up eventually," Sally sneers in Diane's direction.

"Do you know when Mr. Hambler found out about all of this?"

I sit up and try to tune out the antics of the courtroom's ghosts. Oh, did I not mention that? There are two ghosts here, and they're mocking everything that Sally says and does. It's entertaining, but this is the answer I've been waiting weeks for.

"I think he was suspicious from the beginning. But eventually, yeah, he stopped investigating the disappearances too closely. Kept claiming they were runaways and drug addicts. I don't think he wanted to know the truth. Plus, he's always been a bit incompetent."

"When was the first time Mr. Hambler went to the mine?"

"As far as I know, his first visit was the same one you know about."

The overly packed crowd releases a sigh of relief. Chad might have a reputation for womanizing – which I now realize means he was most likely cheating on his wife long before she disappeared

- but no one wants to believe he is capable of being directly involved in any of this. But is that wishful thinking or the truth?

"But surely, with his son on the island?" the district attorney prods her.

"Nah. See, he didn't know his kid was there. Diane fixed that up good. She told him Dustin visited her, but that he'd already left. She also sent a few fake postcards to make it look like Dustin was taking a time out in Wisconsin. She got that idea from me," Sally beams. "It wasn't until she sent yet another postcard instructing him to come to Isle Royale that he figured everything out."

"Why take the risk of involving him?" the district attorney asks.

"It was time to tie up the loose ends. This was supposed to be our last season," Sally says mournfully. "We would have both disappeared with enough money to retire and buy a new identity. Damn you, Alex!" she shouts at me from the witness stand. "You ruined everything!"

Dustin can't suppress a shocked exhalation. From what I understand, Diane had filled his head with so many stories that he believed everything would continue indefinitely. I imagine the knowledge of how much he was played is hitting him hard. There's probably also a lot of guilt for buying into the idea that sacrificing his dad would have fueled them for years to come.

* * * * *

I don't want to testify about the ghosts, but I end up having no choice. There's a lot of skepticism, of course. Normally, this wouldn't surprise or even bother me. But in a town like this that knew about the missing teens and became lulled into inaction because of the wendigo legend? I'm a bit insulted they thought wendigos might be real but are now having such a hard time believing the truth about ghosts.

As I testify, I remember Mabel the librarian's words. They really were all complicit because they chose to close their eyes to something that should have raised red flags.

As everyone will soon know, some of them were being paid off, some thought the teens had just run away, and a few really, truly believed wendigos – sorry, wendigoag - were stalking the streets. If I believed that, I guess I wouldn't want to go poking my nose too far into something like this, either. Instead of taking the risk of speaking out, everyone chose silence, superstitions, and greed. This collective decision killed dozens of teenage boys. It also killed Wayne.

Sally and Diane will be the only people who ultimately do any jail time. Chad took a plea deal – which means he's no longer sheriff – even though his only real crime was not reporting it when he discovered his wife had faked her own death. Apparently, being terrible at your job isn't a crime, so his failure to investigate the disappearances more closely isn't going to become a legal matter. Besides which, he did earn lots of awards and commendations for successfully solving numerous cases that didn't involve missing teenagers, so he wasn't a complete bust as sheriff.

Every person sitting in this courtroom has some blood on their hands, though. I can't help but wonder how many of them also helped support the illegal drug smuggling operation by smoking or snorting the results of each teen's slave labor.

CHAPTER TWENTY-FOUR

One Week Later

I'm glad this is all finally over. Todd is back with his family. Josh was able to put flowers on his mother's grave. Dustin and Chad are working on their fractured relationship. I know neither of them will ever fully forgive Chad for how much he harassed Terrell, regardless of how justified Chad thought he was at the time. But at least they're trying.

Leslie has her business back, and she's busier than ever. It turns out that her massage studio being the last known residence of the ghost whose determination made everything possible is very profitable. It's now a magnet for locals and tourists, and she seems happy.

The two villains of our story will never be able to hurt anyone again. The jury only deliberated for twenty minutes before returning a guilty verdict on every charge. They'll spend the rest of their lives in prison. The National Park Service has taken steps to prevent this nightmare from ever being repeated. The mine has already been filled in, and there's now security around the island all year.

As for me? Headlines around the globe have proclaimed me "a ghost therapist" and "a sleuth who sees dead people." How original, right? The story about this case caught on like wildfire, and there's even talk of it being turned into a movie. I wonder who will play me? More importantly, I wonder if that will finally turn into a big enough payday to cover my bills.

Chad and I are meeting at the bar in a few minutes to say goodbye. I've been sitting here soaking it all in. The wooden table and chair, the dank atmosphere, and the smell of stale beer. Music swirls around my head, and I can't help but think about dancing with Wayne. I wipe a tear from my cheek just as Chad pulls the heavy door open.

I might be crazy, but I do believe he didn't really know what was going on until that day at Isle Royale. I'll never understand how he justified not placing more of an emphasis on each disappearance, but superstitions and fears run deep.

Speaking of which, papers throughout the U.P. have run a fascinating interview with one of Wayne's students. In it, she describes the historical context of the wendigo legend but makes it clear no one on any of the U.P. reservations believe in such things anymore. It's a relic of a time long gone. I hope the people of Munising can allow it to stay buried this time.

Chad and I embrace. "Thank you, Alex."

"For what?"

"For stopping the madness," he winks at me.

"Wait, what did you just say?"

"Mabel says goodbye."

A warm, knowing smile takes me back to the first time the two of us sat in this bar. I know that becoming aware of ghosts makes it easier for people to see and hear them, so I decide not to ask any follow-up questions. Not on that topic, anyway.

"There is one more thing I really need to know. Why didn't you do anything when you found out Diane was alive?"

He hesitates, then says, "Our marriage had fallen apart years before she faked her own death. She always had her secrets, and I wasn't always faithful." Shame and sorrow fill his face and he looks down, suddenly unable to maintain eye contact.

"I figured if she wanted to restart her life that badly, why not let her? I had no idea what she was up to. I didn't even know for sure she was on Isle Royale until a few weeks ago. I wish I had paid closer attention and gotten Diane some help before her secrets devoured her and those kids."

I can tell the weight of Diane's crimes, along with his inaction, will haunt Chad forever. There are many more things I could say. Instead, I grab his hand and pull him onto the dance floor. We sway together one last time as I enjoy the smell of his cologne and the warmth of another human body. Chad isn't the one, and I'm going to miss Wayne forever. But despite my past and the losses I've incurred solving this mystery, I'm clearly ready to love again.

EPILOGUE

It feels so good to be home. I walk past the massive pile of mail on the entry table and rush to my cat. Riley climbs all over me as I pet him and make embarrassing baby talk.

After he settles down enough to take a nap, I allow myself to sneak a glance at the mail. My cat sitter wasn't kidding when she said I was going to need a bedroom just for mail. I guess being on the news is better than a business card.

One envelope in particular catches my attention. It's oddly-shaped and is postmarked from Paris, France. Impressed and curious, I grab my letter opener and wrest the letter free from its temporary housing.

I feel the familiar tug as I read the typed words. At the bottom is something I never thought I'd see: "Enclosed is a voucher for airfare. Please come as soon as you can, Ms. Bentley. All expenses paid, plus $10,000 if you can help."

All expenses paid? And ten-thousand dollars? I reach for my phone and send a text to my cat sitter.

"Sorry, buddy," I say to the black cat's sleeping form. "It looks like I'll be leaving again in the morning."

Alexa Bentley will return in *Frightened in France: Alexa Bentley Paranormal Mysteries Book Two*.

If you enjoyed *Missing in Michigan*, please post a review on Amazon and Goodreads, and be sure to share it with your book-loving friends!

AUTHOR'S NOTE

Thank you for reading *Missing in Michigan: Alexa Bentley Paranormal Mysteries Book One.* I've written many characters in the past in a variety of genres and tones, but none have ever been as much of a joy to embody as Alexa (Alex) Bentley. I hope you've enjoyed spending time with her as much as I have.

Michigan's Upper Peninsula is a very special place to me. I stayed at a cabin just outside of Munising on my honeymoon, and many of Alexa's experiences were inspired by that wonderful week. For example, my spouse and I saw the Northern Lights there together for the first time on a chilly night in September. The restaurants Alexa visits were also inspired by the wonderful food we had there (especially breakfast!).

As far as I know, there are no ghosts haunting Munising, nor are there any dark secrets or mysteries to solve. But people really did mine Isle Royale six-thousand years ago. The wendigo legend also traces some of its roots to the Native Americans of the Upper Peninsula.

If you're ever in Michigan, I highly recommend visiting the U.P. – and Detroit, of course. :)

Please post a review to Amazon and Goodreads if you enjoyed this book. Reviews and any other form of word-of-mouth (including social media postings) are an invaluable way of supporting your favorite indie authors. I am forever grateful to all of you who have supported my books in the past, and your continued support is greatly appreciated!

If you have any questions or feedback, please feel free to reach out to me via my website or social media. Thank you!

Facebook - https://www.facebook.com/aprilataylorhorror/
Twitter - https://twitter.com/aprilataylor
Instagram - https://www.instagram.com/aprilataylorwriter/
My Website - https://aprilataylor.net
Goodreads -
https://www.goodreads.com/author/show/17756638.April_A_T
aylor
Amazon - https://www.amazon.com/April-A.-
Taylor/e/B07B48G36N

ACKNOWLEDGEMENTS

Tina, Christina, Patty, and Anne – Thank you for being the first readers to meet Alexa Bentley. Your feedback was very helpful and greatly appreciated! You're all awesome!

Anne – Thank you for your constant encouragement and support, and for listening to me talk nonstop about writing and books. Thanks also for always asking the tough questions and pointing out things I would have missed. Missing in Michigan is much better because of you, as are all of my other books.

Kristen – Thank you for helping to inspire Alexa Bentley's profession and for providing valuable input on some of the book's psychological themes.

Riley – My writing and editing buddy is the inspiration for Alexa's cat, Riley. Thanks, Mister Man. Want to see the real-life Riley? Check out Instagram (@aprilataylorwriter)!

You – Thank you for reading this book!

www.ingramcontent.com/pod-product-compliance
Lightning Source LLC
Chambersburg PA
CBHW021104130626
46554CB00002B/522